SPICES
ARE SWEET

by DD

FROG BOOKS

First published in India 2012 by Frog Books
An imprint of Leadstart Publishing Pvt Ltd
1 Level, Trade Centre
Bandra Kurla Complex
Bandra (East) Mumbai 400 051 India
Telephone: +91-22-40700804
Fax: +91-22-40700800
Email: info@leadstartcorp.com
www.leadstartcorp.com / www.frogbooks.net

Sales Office:
Unit: 122 / Building B/2
First Floor, Near Wadala RTO
Wadala (East) Mumbai 400 037 India
Phone: +91-22-24046887

US Office:
Axis Corp, 7845 E Oakbrook Circle
Madison, WI 53717 USA

Copyright © DD

All rights reserved. No part of this publication may be reproduced, stored in or introduced into a retrieval system, or transmitted, in any form, or by any means (electronic, mechanical, photocopying, recording or otherwise) without the prior written permission of the publisher. Any person who does any unauthorised act in relation to this publication may be liable to criminal prosecution and civil claims for damages.

ISBN 978-93-81836-51-4

Book Editor: Cora Bhatia
Design Editor: Mishta Roy

Typeset in Book Antiqua
Printed at Repro India Ltd, Mumbai

Price — India: Rs 125; Elsewhere: US $5

Dedication

Kumar for making everything work.

"You can have it all. Just not all at once."
— Oprah Winfrey

About the Author

DD is an avid reader who loves to blog. She gave up her medical school to discover her destiny. DD aspired to live in her pyjamas and watch Oprah all day; luckily, her soul mate discovered her writing talent. She lives in Colombo with her husband, two kids and loves the fact that she is from an island. DD trades in spices, learns Spanish, and is ready to give parental advice at all times to all moms. She can be found writing plots, for her novel ideas, at all other times.DD is happy to state that she has found her soul mate in an arranged marriage.

Acknowledgements

To the ones who held my hand and walked along with me:

Thanks to the love of my life Kumar, for believing in me, his patience in my writing at all moments. This book is dedicated to you!

Divya and Venky for making my life complete. Mom, dad, Shanker, and Shankari who are always a part of me.

Swarup and Omkar from Leadstart publishing for giving me a break. My editor Cora Bhatia, for fine-tuning my manuscript, you are amazing. Mishta and Sirawon for their design and time.

Roshini for the laughter and the phone calls, Namini for encouragement. Gotham Online New York, especially Andrea for making the writing better, Mrs. T of Wycherley for making me love English and Reading.

Athai, Mama, Raja, Murali, Murugan and Anitha.

Meena, Prathima, Priya D and the bloggers who have taken the time to read my work, I love you

The friends who share my daily laughter and you guys know who you are. My extended family of cousins, in laws who have so much to say, you guys rock.

Prologue

"This is a sacred thread. This is essential for my long life. I tie this around your neck, O maiden having many auspicious attributes! May you live happily for a hundred years with me!"

- *The verse, which is said when tying the "Thali" thread in a south Indian wedding.*

Hindu weddings have been a union of a man and woman to commit to live a life of harmony. It is believed that the two souls will live, be united, and reunited, in all their after lives. So, yes they are indeed fixed in heaven. The rituals are followed under religious guidance, performed by a priest.

Pre-wedding

Nichiyathartham: The bride's family hosts an engagement ceremony for close relatives. The engagement is a colourful affair, whereby an elder in the family would announce the date of the wedding. The groom's family would provide gifts to the bride such as saris, jewellery and sweets. The bride's family would in turn present similar gifts. The parents would exchange a platter of betel leaves, coconuts, fruits, *Kumkum* (vermillion) and sandalwood paste to confirm the engagement.

The groom's family would buy the bride her wedding sari and reception sari, as the bride's family would buy the wedding attire and suit for the groom. The close relatives of the couple are also bought new clothes to mark the occasion by their respective sides. A team of relatives are sent to invite the guests to grace the occasion.

Hindu wedding retinue:

- Bride
- Groom
- Bride's parents
- Groom's parents
- Bride's maternal uncle
- Groom's Maternal Uncle
- Bride's brother/ male cousin to accompany the groom
- Grooms Sister/ Female Cousin to accompany the bride
- Relatives of the bride and groom
- Friends of the bride and groom

Wedding Day

Fresh plantain trees with fruit tied on either side of the entrance, a string of mango leaves and pine petals are connected in between. This symbolizes an auspicious start to live a life of evergreen abundance for generations to come.

The floor is decorated with a beautiful *Kolam*, by women to mark the auspicious wedding. The elaborate details worked carefully are a treat for the eyes.

Relatives of the groom and bride await to welcome the guests with a tray offering, sandalwood paste, *kumkum*(vermillion) to place on the forehead and sugar candy to mark sweetness in life. The guests are showered with rose water to perfume them.

The notes of the *nathaswaram* and *melam* play in harmony, to welcome the guests.

A wedding is an occasion for all the near and distant relatives, friends, neighbours to come together to attend and bless the couple.

The groom is welcomed by the bride's family and her relatives into the wedding hall.

'Ganapathi/ GaneshaPooja': The first ritual is to pray to Lord Ganesha to remove any obstacles for the day or in their life and also to bless the couple.

The priest would create a sacred *fire homam* within a closed area where by the fire god is present to bless the ceremony.

Married Women from the family would decorate the pillars with turmeric and *kumkum* (vermilion) dots. The bride's family would soak nine different pulses in vessels, for them to sprout. The Sprouting of the pulses symbolizes nurturing and growing of a new relationship. The sprouts would be maintained until the marriage and dissolved in a river or sea, three days later.

The wedding ceremony is mostly conducted in Sanskrit, a holy language of devotion. Different castes, families and cultures in Hinduism have made their own depiction of the wedding ceremony. The basic rituals performed and vows taken would be similar.

The families of the bride and the groom would sit and face each other as the priest chants prayers to seek blessings to the couple. The names of the families of three generations of ancestors are read and prayed for.

KannikaDhanam: The bride's hand is placed in the groom's right palm, by the bride's father. As the groom is entrusted with her hand, it is a symbol that he is responsible to look after her in joy, sorrow and at all times in life.

MangalyaDharanam: The *"Thali"* is a yellow thread coated with turmeric, bearing a gold pendant; it plays a significant part in the ceremony, as would a ring in the western wedding.

The *Thali* would be taken around in a plate bearing betel leaves and given to all the guests to be touched and blessed.

The tying of the thread would be done at the auspicious time, whereby the bride would face eastwards and the groom would

10 *Spices Are Sweet*

tie one knot, and his sister would tie two knots of the thread behind her neck. The groom's sister or a female cousin would hold a lit lamp behind the neck.

The priests would chant the verse:

"This is a sacred thread. This is essential for my long life. I tie this around your neck O maiden having many auspicious attributes. May you live happily for hundred years (with me)."

The bride and the groom would be showered with turmeric coated raw rice and flowers petals as a token of blessings, by the guests.

GettiMellam: The *nathashwaram* and *Melam* would play the special music loudly, to ward off any inauspicious sounds. It also directs the Guests attention to the ceremony.

Kumkum / Vermillion: A red powder is applied on the parting of the hair (forehead) of the bride by the bridegroom, for the first time. This is significant to show that the bride is married

Chapter 1 - TEA

When we were kids, we were fed with food, religion and one more line thrown in like a prayer, "You will have an arranged marriage and your parents will select the chosen one." So we were not allowed to date. My parents would find the match and make it happen when the time was right.

Dooms day came earlier than expected, when my mom was screaming at me to wake up. I woke up to see mom in a frenzy her eyes were really bright. "They are coming," she said repeatedly and did a little dance. Watching my mom in her extremely bright purple sari doing a little jig was like watching Barney. My aunties, the workers, and all the women folk of the village were in my room. Holy shit I am in a dream. Women are still chattering.

I forgot to introduce myself. My name is Santhoshi (which means happy, terribly, really lacking at this point) 25years, living in an Indian Village. When I say village the picture is of cows, buffaloes, a random elephant, paddy fields and a large Indian family with about 100 family members. Later in the story, you will meet my family members. Oh, before I forget I am an ordinary girl with average looks, but my family thinks otherwise.

Grandma holds my face and looks at me dreamily. "Thank god we fixed your teeth when you were a teenager. I cannot see any flaw in your face."

Mom and grandma have hit the bottle I am sure. Their tea has been spiked with alcohol.

My aunt sniffles and has tears in her eyes, "you are going my child."

That is how my day started with a bang. I was being sent to the *guillotine of bride viewing.* It was a beautiful enough sunny day, but the darkness in my head was a contrast to the happenings. Therefore, I had to bathe and get ready. I was dressed in my aunt's lucky sari, intensely colourful attire with prominent white and red roses. Apparently, my uncle said yes, when he saw my aunt and this is the lucky charm. I looked a mess, a bulky ugly bouquet. My aunt tied my hair into a braid and adorned it with flowers. Jasmine my favourite flowers to be exact. The makeup, put on by a lucky cousin who was hitched at first sight, made me age another five years. The house was a beehive of activity, where the cooking for the tea party was being carried out at high speed. .

"So who is it grandma?" I asked.

Grandma was busy reading her prayer books and making vows in her head that I should be hitched.

"Your aunt did you see her cry, she is jealous that it's you and not her daughter."

"Who is coming today grandma?" I repeat clearly and loudly.

"They will say yes my dear, no doubt," rants grandma. Seriously, she needs her hearing checked.

Therefore, I walk out and repeat the question to my mom.

"Do not worry they will say yes," echoes my mother and she holds my face, and looks deeply into my eyes.

I was horrified and had to move away. Why does the family have their own conversation? Some strange man is coming into my house with his family, to check me out, as if I am a prized cow and eat all our food.

My cousins had turned up and were planning their outfits for the engagement and the rest of the wedding rituals. They had the gossip, and exchanged news for some of my DVDs the guy is a USA return trophy catch (this means a person who has gone to the states and completed a degree there) and the family is loaded with extra cash. No, wonder the women folk were in frenzy they had mistaken this Indian dude to be Brad Pitt.

My dad and uncles come home, engrossed in their usual man

talk, ignoring the buzz in the house. The man talk clearly consisted of the plantation, labour trouble, the drought or rain (add in whichever suits the weather). They usually have this conversation without fail, every single time they meet. This means essentially every day.

"Brother we have trouble with labourer S; he has been stealing stocks every day. I think he has another key," says uncle.

"Be patient, he has a family to support," answers dad. "It's better to have a known devil than an unknown angel."

"You know he is a devil, we should send him home," bellows uncle.

"How are the rains?" continues dad.

"No crops for the season," responds uncle.

If someone is not stealing all the paddy, then there is no rain. If it rains, then it floods. You honestly cannot have enough of it.

I was given tea and snacks, which I ate with my cousins and listened to their chattering.

"Will we get new clothes for Santhoshi's wedding?" asks Cousin No 1

"We will all get new clothes of course!" screams cousin No 2.

"We should go on a holiday to celebrate her wedding to Chennai," continues Cousin No 1.

Seriously, I do not see the relevance of us all going to the city to celebrate, that too after taxing my parents for new clothes, but my cousins are making skilful use of the fact that I was getting married.

The arrival of the visitors was greeted with an excited silence. I was not allowed to the guest's room yet. My cousins were running in and out and giving reports that he looked like a movie star.

My mom rushed into the room, her eyes were glowing again. I prayed in my mind do not do the jig. She told me when I step out to clasp my hands and pray in the general direction of the visitors, as a mark of respect and keep my head bowed. This

14 *Spices Are Sweet*

must be the hundredth time I hear this instruction. Over the years, I have seen this in several Indian movies, as well as when my cousins or relatives got married.

It was time; I paraded to the living room, with a flock of cousins surrounding me, to see the intruders. I looked up; it was a blur .I saw many women, a few men, and quickly did the prayer thing. "Sit down," she said. The voice was from the woman, who was wearing the most dazzling sari, and all her jewellery, the groom's mom. Barney, sorry mom, was no match to this tyrannosaurus. I looked at my mom, and she did the head-nodding thing. Indians have this symbolic sign of doing plenty of head nodding instead of conversation. We nod our heads for yes, for no, for how are you, and you just nod, your head back saying yes, no, I am OK get a life!

There was a flurry. I was made to sit next to the woman. I could feel all eyes on me. I now know how the animals in the zoo felt.

"So can you cook?" she asked.

"She almost entered '*Master Chef India*,'" mom broke in instantly.

"She can sew, she can drive, she can swim, she can sing," my aunt listed.

"Come dear lord Krishna," my grandma is singing.

She is quickly shut up with a fierce look from mom. I cannot swim, because I have never been to a swimming class. When I sing, the frogs might jump out of the pond and join me. My cooking; oh well let us just say, I managed to send my brother to emergency, after he ate the cake I baked.

"What are your hobbies?" questioned another fierce one.

"She collects stamps!" mom said proudly.

Oh god, open up the ground and swallow me.

"Oh can we have a look at it?" asks the fierce one.

Checkmate mom, I wonder how she is going to get out of that one. Mom actually clicks her finger and my aunt brings a hefty album I had never seen. Since I had my head bowed, this was with eye coordination from the side of my eyes that I saw this little miracle happening. I wonder where mom stole this.

"I would like to talk to her alone if I may have permission," a man asked.

I looked up at the direction of the voice. There, he was the man of my dreams, except he looked like any other guy to me. There was quick head shaking between my our relatives, and eyebrow waggling, and silent conversation with no words coming out.

"We are very modern in our thinking, they should talk. Even I spoke to my husband when we first met," said the fierce one.

She gave another fierce once over at her husband, who was sitting with a blank expression on his face. I do not think the man even blinked his eyes.

"Yes we are the new age, we are watching star TV and CNN these days," mom says.

Oh, cringe (new age? Where does mom come up with these phrases from)? I look at my dad who looks flustered. This is so not part of his intent, where we talk alone. Everyone proceeds to get up and direct us to the dining room. I stand there only a few yards away, from the rest of the group, where everyone can eavesdrop.

I look at Ashok; he looks distinctly uncomfortable. He points at the garden, which opens out to the back yard and asks permission from my grandmother, if we could go there. Grandma does a swooning thing to fall into his arms. Aunt directly intervenes and holds grandma. Quick head nodding from my dad and I follow him into the garden.

16 *Spices Are Sweet*

Chapter 2 - Sweet

"Can you speak English?" Ashok asked, as soon as we stepped into the garden.

I was speechless (this seems to be happening to me too often these days) and looked at him. Ashok was peering at grandma's money plant (a plant with a palm shaped leaf, which grows like a climber, a belief that the plant attracts money). It was clear at that moment that this man had no clue about me, he had not read by Bio Data (the little A4 Sheet with my entire academic and horoscope background on it; or a sheet screaming For Sale). I know English, French and a handful of Indian languages. I had completed my Bachelor's in Economics from one of the best Universities in India.

Ashok turned around from peering at the plant and looked at me. I did not feel my heart flutter or my stomach turn. I felt nothing. I did my head nodding (nod nod nod).

"Listen, I will tell you this once clearly, I have a girlfriend and my family does not know yet. I want you to go back and tell your parents that you don't like me," he said.

Uhm, what sorry did I just hear that?

I did the eyebrow-waggling thing. I am very confused with this turn of events, for god sake I am a small-town girl from India. I did not know what the protocol for this kind of thing was. Ashok sighed loudly and repeated his sentence.

"What do I tell my parents, they will not tolerate I don't like you," I replied.

This piece was true, highly traditional Indian parents are not satisfied with the statement; I did not like him. I grew up with the motto, when you meet the man your parents pick; you have no choice but to say yes.

"You have to tell them you don't like me or I will tell my parents you have a boy friend," he said, and there, I could see the resemblance of T- Rex.

This man was blackmailing me, and I was certainly not sure if my family would believe me. Let me correct that again; mom would surely trust him.

He just walked off back into the house, and I was left there in a daze. I walked back in shock. The thing about Indian families is they *love you to bits*, as long as you do things their way. There should be a guide for this kind of situation. I walked in and saw all the eager faces smiling at me in joy. Ashok's family was ready to leave, after plenty of head nodding and promises to be in touch. I kept my head down right through. What do I tell my parents?

"Your names match!" my mom shrieked into my ear.

"We will look at dates, as they will surely say yes," boomed my uncle. The chatter increased tenfold.

Suddenly a piece of laddu (a sweet made of flour, sugar and butter) was stuffed into my mouth by my aunt. I could choke with the sweetness and the calorie counts on that. This is another typical Indian practice, where they stuff calorie dense sweets into your mouth, when they think there is fabulous news.

"We will go to the temple," said grandma and picked up her flower basket, with a twinkle in her eye.

God bless grandma. So off, we went to the temple, which was a ten-minute walk.

"When your grandfather came to see me," she started.

Now all the women in the house filled us repeatedly about their bride viewing. It is identically the same; man comes, looks at the woman, eats up the food, and says yes and then the wedding. We went to the temple and prayed in silence.

I looked at the stone statue of Lord Ganesha (the elephant faced

18 *Spices Are Sweet*

god who is supposed to help you in tough times). I thought, dear Lord help me out of this one, for I am a mere mortal and am terribly confused of what to say or do.

On our way back, we saw a funeral procession, where the corpse is carried by the men of the family, on a small platform, decorated with flowers, to the burial ground. At the cemetery, the body is burnt according to Hindu customs. This is not a happy omen now, I thought.

As if she could read my mind grandma said, "It is a telling sign, seeing a corpse, as when your grandpa came to see me."

Seriously, it couldn't have been the same body now?

The sight that greeted grandma and me at home was of tragedy. Mom was crying, with the aunts around her. The men looked pissed off. What is next I wondered?

"Our lovely girl will be going away that is why the family is sad. We can visit her," announced grandma.

I looked around in confusion and mom ran up to me, hugged me and cried out, "I knew he was not a good enough match for you, that family looked vicious!"

"We will stop him on his way and break his car and his legs," shouted uncle. My aunt jumped up to stop him, along with the rest of the relatives.

The house turned into madness, mayhem, there were too many conversations, and grandma looked as lost as I did. Mom was weeping in despair.

"You should have told us when they were there," said dad and shook his head and walked off.

Am I missing a point here? I wondered to myself.

Grandma and I were quickly shoved into two chairs, and updated on the happenings. My nine-year-old cousin, Krish, had been eavesdropping on the courting conversation. He had repeated it to the bigger cousin, who in turn had repeated it to the fifth cousin and so on, until the 10th cousin. Anyway, within ten minutes my uncle had called up Ashok's parents and screamed murder.

I was extremely tired and went to bed. I could hear my aunt and grandma discussing me, which was interrupted by the arrival of my elder sister Nandini. I have not introduced my family yet, my grandma, dad, mom, my older sister Nandini, my younger brother Anish. I heard Nandini yell at my mom and then silence. Mom probably was updating her on the happenings in the house.

Nandini was not invited for the bride viewing; to put it lightly, she is a devilishly complex person. She was married at the age of 21, but ten years later, she still turns up at my parents and rips them off with her demands. I could hear her tell my mom that I could marry her brother in law, who according to me is a scumbag. The few times I had met him at a festival or wedding; he would stare at me lecherously and scratch his balls.

I must have fallen asleep at some point in the night. I woke up to the fragrance of jasmine, rose and musk. I am dreaming again. Nope there was a splash of cold water on my face. My best friend Maya was sitting on my bed.

"Babes surprised," she said.

"Oh Maya, welcome to the madness," I replied.

Maya had called mom last night and got the update, since I had forgotten to call her. She had come to whisk me away to the city. In these exceptional circumstances, she had cleverly pointed out to mom that I need a change of the scene. The plan was to take me to her house, where there were no unknown men, except her dad. The only reason for this sudden escape was the turn of events. My parents were very strict in not allowing me to stay over at a friend's house, having seen a number of movies where a girl stays at friend's house and meets a boy, heaven forbid now we don't want a love marriage, which has never happened in generations do we? I normally would not have gotten approval for this sort of escape, given the number of events all were keen to see me leave, except Nandini. She just sat there and stared at me with disdain. You know, how you have a great sister, and she loves you to bits, in my case, it was the exact opposite. I am still trying to figure that one out.

We had breakfast with grandma, who was entertaining us with stories from the sixties. Mom had a puffed up face and puffy

20 *Spices Are Sweet*

eyes. Tragedy had silenced her for the moment. I went to say good-bye to dad.

He gave me a bundle of money and said, "Take care Santhoshi, I want you to come back in two days, your flight ticket will be ready in Bangalore."

We got into Maya's car. Mani had a disinterested look. He is Maya's driver, cook and one-man army. We left with loads of byes from all the neighbours. I was the scandal of the village, the girl who was ditched at the bride viewing. The news must have spread like wild fire, since the whole village knew that there was an incident in the house. Oh well!

I started stripping in the car. I saw Mani view from the mirror. He was so used to this. Before I forget, I stripped my Indian clothes, because I had been wearing my jeans and t-shirt underneath. I let out my hair from its tight braid. I opened my compact and checked my makeup.

"You are such a loser," Maya said.

I am used to Maya's screaming and shouting that I should be myself. I ignored her and opened the bottle of wine stashed under the seat. After one month, the first sip was getting me high. Yes, there is no drinking allowed in my house, in the village. Everyone is a teetotaller at my house. I had picked this delightful habit from our university days.

"Maya give me a break, don't u want to listen to what happened," I asked.

"No, I think you should tell your family to allow you to complete your Masters get a job and stop this   nonsense of looking for guys. You should also check out a few of the guys from our college," Maya said.

I drank silently, ate some cookies, and dosed off for the long drive. Maya took me home, and her parents were there. I love aunt, Maya's mom. Uncle scared me to bits. Uncle had a bit of a thing about himself, he stresses several times, about how many people he knew.

He would say," Maya my pet, your dad is a man who knows many people," and stare at us as if to make a point.

This is one of many of his eccentricities. I do not know why, but I would roll around laughing, repeating his words, and laugh some more, when we were alone. Maybe, I had a strange sense of humour or something.

Chapter 3 - Ginger

During my two days stay, Maya's dad was not around, as he was away travelling. My two friends, Priya and Karthik came to see me. Priya is from Hyderabad, a large city in India. She is a villager at heart, who lives in a city.

"At some point in our life our roles were reversed," we joked.

Karthik, four years our senior, is the one who holds a job, and should be the responsible adult in our click. I met Priya and Maya at college, in my first year. Karthik entered the picture quite unexpectedly, when he was going out with one of our friends Anu. Their relationship broke down, with Anu two-timing Karthik, but our friendship survived with him.

My friendship with Karthik was sealed at the time, when we were sharing a drink and realised that we were also from the same community. The world certainly is extremely small, so we laugh and gossip often. Karthik too had gone for a bride viewing, so we had to compare notes.

"Santhoshi I went to see your distant cousin Vidya," he said and put his head down.

"You idiot! You told me it was some girl from Vizag I wouldn't know!" I hit him with the magazine.

Vidya is my long lost cousin, the daughter of the third sister of my aunt's cousin's. We usually, do not talk to the family, due to a feud, details of which I do not recollect. I think it was something terribly significant; like forgetting to invite my aunt's pet parrot, for a naming ceremony.

I noticed that Maya and Priya had disappeared and I was left alone. So they had known, and I was left in the dark. I will kill them when they come back.

"I said yes, the engagement is next month and the wedding is in July," he said.

He looked up, and I saw how difficult it must have been to say this. We both kept looking at each other silently for a minute. Wait a minute, why are we staring at each other. Oh yes, I am in line next.

I started laughing, and kept laughing. You see sometimes that I am rather on a looney edge. Maya and Priya crept back into the room.

"I am happy for you, congratulations, Vidya has scary ogling eyes, but she is ok. I played with her when I was a kid," I said.

I threw the cushion at Maya, and we ended up with a cushion fight. We went to our favourite Chinese restaurant Ginger for dinner, to celebrate Karthik's engagement, and my escape. We laughed so much, making fun of everyone in the restaurant.

There was a young couple playing footsie under the table. We kept looking down under the table so many times, that they moved tables.

I think, I still remember how much we laughed even today, because it would be one of the last moments, that we would all laugh so much in our adult lives.

I was to leave the next morning; Karthik had gone back. Maya and Priya were grilling me about Vidya. I could remember the last time, I had seen her was when I was ten years old, at yet another wedding. She was the most competitive girl I had met. At that little age, she would give me the once over (look at me from top to bottom and stare). She would grab my skirt and ask, how much? She would ask me about my school progress card, and she would demand to know everything that I had been doing. Her nonstop questioning was a tad tedious for me and I would trip her and win every game that we played. Vidya would burst out crying and scream foul play. I would laugh at her face and take off. I would get my brother to fart and scream that Vidya had farted. She would cry some more.

24 *Spices Are Sweet*

To put it lightly, I may not be at the top of her top favourite list at that time. Many years later, I am sure she would have grown up. I did an impression of her eyes and we cracked up laughing.

"I don't like the sound of her, she seems like a spoilt brat," Maya said.

"We were all spoilt brats when we were kids," I responded.

We looked at Priya, shrieked out in laughter, and screamed "Except Priya!"

"I hate you donkeys!" screamed Priya.

We mocked her and shrieked in laughter.

My two days with my friends just flew by eating, shopping, watching movies and a visit to the spa. I was relaxed, rejuvenated and it was time to go home. Mani drove us to the airport and he had tears in his eyes when he dropped me.

"Don't Cry Mani I will be back," I said.

"I am not crying Santhoshi, some dust in my eyes,"he scoffed back. Oh well I should have known, he would not exactly be weeping that I was leaving; he must be relieved.

"Be yourself silly old cow; tell them, you want to read a masters and find a job!" Maya said.

I just nodded and hugged her good bye. I was lugging my luggage, when Karthik came rushing in, his hair a mess, his tie askew.

"Will you come for the engagement?" he asked.

"I don't think my parents will let me Karthik, I'll try for the wedding. I have not even told them that I have a best friend, who is a guy, who also happens to be from our community," I said.

"They will be so scandalised," I continued.

"I want you to be there," he said.

"I shall bring her," said Maya.

I hugged them goodbye and left. I thought of Ashok, I wondered if his parents agreed to the girl, he was in love with. If he had been single, would I too be celebrating my engagement? I shook my head and the thoughts away. No one asked me about my two days with my friends. I had nothing to say about it, so it was confusing why I was thinking of this now.

I felt a few stares; and turned to look at some passengers stare at me pointedly. What now? Oh, yes my mobile screaming, Madonna's tune "Like a Virgin!" I quickly turned it off (I must remember to switch the tune to something decent like ring ring before getting on the flight).

"Are you at the airport?" mom asked.

"Yes mom, I am fine, how are you? I have missed the flight," I said.

"You can't miss the flight your poor mother will have a heart attack?" mom shrieked.

"I am kidding, I will be there in the next two hours," I said.

"Are you wearing a nice *Shalwar Kameez* (Indian clothes), you must go to the temple on the way to the airport!" she continued.

"Yes mom, I am wearing shorts and t-shirt!" I said.

I had to hear her scream and yell about how difficult it is to bring up kids.

"Are you wearing a nice Indian *Shalwar Kameez* (Indian Clothes)?" shouted grandma on the phone.

"Yes grand ma, I am," I said.

Grandma cut off the mobile, after screaming to the whole house that she is dressed respectably. I think the passengers heard grandma, I saw a mom stare at me and grab her two kids and walk away. The boarding for my flight was announced. I sat and looked out of the window.

"Hi I am Vikram, Call me Vik," a voice announced.

I turned around to look at the most stunning man standing there, his hands stretched out. I was dumbstruck with the vision before me. It's a Greek God; nope it's a Greek Indian God. Wow, how come I had not seen this beauty at the airport?

26 *Spices Are Sweet*

He waved his hands slowly. I swallowed and quickly shook hands with him.

"We are extremely sorry, the flight is delayed for five minutes, due to circumstances beyond our control," the announcement came over the PTA.

"Oh bugger, my parents will be panicking," Vikram said. "So, we will have to have a chat I guess..."

I could just sit and stare at this guy all day I think. I introduced myself quickly, and that started our conversation. Vikram was hilarious and soon we were laughing and chatting away like old friends.

Our pleasant conversation was stopped by the insistent ring of his mobile. He picked it up, and it was rude, but I had to listen into his conversation. It was a guy at the other end, who was screaming at Vikram, the poor guy was trying hard to pacify him.

"How could you do this Vik?" he shouted.

"No I will be there soon, I will explain. Just calm down," Vikram Said.

Work related, I guessed cleverly. Vikram worked for a large garment factory designing clothes, but his parents thought he was trading in clothes. I could understand as, it's easier to tell everyone I sell a product, not I design it, and they would always appreciate selling to design.

" ($*" (*) $)" ("), he shouted.

"I love you," Vikram said seriously.

Wait did he just say he loves me.? That was quick. He will be proposing to me quickly. We will have such marvellous looking kids. I must respond I did a turn to look at Vikram; he was still on the phone. God Indian men can be so gay sometimes, saying I love you to their male friends. I thought Vikram did look too good to be true. He hung up his mobile and looked quite sad.

The PTA announced the '*take off*," of our flight, twenty minutes later.

Chapter 4 - Coffee

The flight landed, a solid forty-five minutes later than the estimated time. Domestic flights, I tell you.

I came out of the airport to find a group of the family outside, my brother, a cousin brother and an aunt.

"Welcome committee?" I asked my brother Anish.

He just nodded with no expression, my cousin and aunt nodded their heads. My aunt was giving me the once over very seriously. Stare, check, stare and check. I looked down, to see if I had forgotten to wear my pants. Nope, they were there all right.

I wondered why a part of the family had turned up. Usually it is the driver, or sometimes one family member who comes to pick me up.

"Where is mom?" I asked.

Everyone looked at each other and said, "home" together.

"I thought we were going to the temple with mom," I asked again.

Everyone looked at each other and did not reply. I got into the car, which was tooting loudly. Oh well I just looked out to the start of the dried up area of a field. The barren land and dried up trees stared back at me. Idly my mind thought, they need some water.

My brother Anish is eighteen years old, just finished his high school. He is a shy person. I think he is not sure about me, because he randomly asks me questions like, "Did you see the city party in college?" or "You did not get a boyfriend now did

28 *Spices Are Sweet*

you?" I would hoot in laughter, say yes and he would shake his head saying no. He is a good-hearted person.

I turned towards my aunt and looked at her, she had her face turned the other way. She seemed remarkably quiet. I guess, they have not gotten over the tragic bride viewing. Well have I got over it? I was not sure what I felt. Confused was one thing. I had always thought the prince charming would come, see me, and I would be married immediately. I am sure; I would have adjusted, except I would have missed the occasional glass of wine. I would miss the partying. I would miss the city life. Maybe, I would get married into the city, then I could sneak all this in. How would I sneak partying in? This was all a bit too much for my little brain to process.

"Stop the car, we should get some jasmine flowers for Santhoshi's hair," my aunt said.

The driver stepped on the brakes and stopped the car just before it hit a cow right in the middle of a road. We had reached the village and there on the roadside near the temple, the flower vendor was seated. My brother hurriedly jumped out of the car and rushed to buy flowers.

My hair shampooed, conditioned and blow-dried to the maximum, this morning screamed out in protest. I don't want any flowers now. I try not to figure out why this sudden need to adorn my hair. Then, my brother comes back with enough flowers for half the village. My aunt quickly tries to pull my hair, braid it hurriedly. My hair does not give way; I mean, I spent half-hour on it this morning. No blow-dried perfect hair is a match for your aunt's hands. She wanted a braid and a half a ton of flowers in there. Well that's what she is going to get. After a bit of a struggle and half the flowers in my hair, we reach the lane leading to our house. There is a new vehicle in front of the house.

"Who has come home?" I ask Anish.

He looks at my aunt, my cousin and does that shifty thing again. My aunt quickly grabs my handbag and hurries into the house. I rush after her for my handbag; it is my priced Designer Bag. I don't want her to be throwing it around, in the dust and cow dung.

I hear voices laughing and talking loudly, especially mom's voice is an octave or two higher. Inside there are three strangers and my relatives in the living room. My aunt nudges me to do the prayer thing. Therefore, that's what I do.

"Sit down my child," she said. I looked at the woman with the most beautiful serene face. She was wearing a simple, elegant blue sari. The gentleman by her side was smart and had a big smile on his face. I sat down.

"Do not be afraid, your parents must have told you. It is only right we introduce ourselves, we are from the SM family and our son will be here in few minutes. We are on a courtesy visit, if you and my son agree we will be the happiest parents," she said.

I looked at my mom, she looked like the cat that had the cream and was quick to interrupt and ask them about some long lost relative. My dad was talking to the uncle, my grand ma was trying to butt into the conversation between the women.

I observed all this and thought to myself, why so quickly. I have not had time to recover yet. At the same time, these parents of the boy look like a dream come true.

Aunt SM said, "You must be tired child, why don't you have something to drink maybe some filter coffee?"

I just nodded my head to say no it's ok. I saw my aunts and mom give a nod of approval at this. They had forgotten to feed me and some stranger was suggesting that I have my coffee. My family was thrilled with this. Oh God!

Quickly, I was given a cup of filter coffee, a plate of food containing onion rings and laddu again. I politely said no to my aunt.

Filter coffee in South India is one of the most delicious brewed drinks. My mornings usually kick starts with one. It gives you a sense of comfort when you sip the concoction. Filter coffee is made in a special silver filter, which is a two-tier vessel, with a filter on top. The freshly ground powder, bought as it is ground every week, is filtered to this delicious strong coffee, with milk and sugar. It has to be served piping hot in a tiny silver cup. The silver cup is extra heavy weight to hold the heat. If the

30 *Spices Are Sweet*

coffee burnt your tongue, you would be sued if you were living elsewhere, but this was a sign of a budding relationship in our part of the world.

The filter has to be fresh and it will be the biggest crime, if the powder, which has been used, is recycled to make coffee. The recycling of the coffee concoction is done to discourage unwanted relatives from entering your house. So if the guest is not your favourite, just give them recycled coffee from your leftover powder in the filter.

The new visitors here were definitely being served the best of the best. Special filter coffee made with freshly ground coffee beans, milk from the cows and special sugar from the sugarcane fields.

"Go inside and have a cup my child, it is ok we will talk to your parents," SM said.

I love this woman already; she was saying all the right things. I smiled at her, nodded my thanks and went into the kitchen. The three maids surrounded me and grinned in delight.

"SM Family, they are so rich," said maid number one.

"SM family makes crackers you will be just two villages away," said the maid number two.

"Their son is in the city," said my aunt who had appeared out of thin air.

"Please wash your face; I will put some make up for you."

"No aunt, let me handle this please," I said and rushed off upstairs into my room.

I went into my room and plopped myself in front of my mirror. Will this face sell this time? My face seemed to ask. The thudding on my door had me up, even before I could answer the question. Anish my brother was outside.

"I am sorry, I should have warned you, but amma said that you will be upset, unhappy and it would show in your face. They seem really nice. I am dreadfully sorry," he said sheepishly, scratched his head, and looked about.

DD 31

"Oh well I will remember this and find you a charming girl, who oils her hair, and puts on an inch of powder when it's your time Anish," I said.

My brother burst out laughing, and so did I. I could hear grandma calling my name from downstairs.

"Get me five minutes Anish," I said.

My brother jumped a stair apart happily. I smiled, watching him. It was time to apply the war paint and get ready.

I was ready ten minutes later; I had even changed into a simple cotton sari. I loved my parents. I am sure they will be pleased that I am making the effort. I looked into the mirror. Yes, I liked what I saw.

I went down the stairs and into the living room. There was a moment of silence, when I walked in. I looked at papa and amma; they looked so happy and proud. SM aunt got up, and came up to me, and did a gesture, where they take their palms around in circles and keep it in their forehead. An Indian custom to ward off evil eyes.

"She is indeed beautiful, sit down!" she said.

"We are very sorry that our son is late, but he should be here any minute," uncle SM said.

"He can take his own time, we have so much to talk," mom replied. Really, mom could be over bearing at times.

"We do this prayer singing every week at the temple," grandma announced. Oh, lord now she wanted to do one of her performances.

"Oh look at the time we must light the lamp, come amma," she said taking grandma to the prayer room and averting the disaster of her singing.

SM aunt casually questioned me about college days and as I was explaining to her, we heard a car come. Papa, my uncle and Anish rushed out to welcome the new visitor. Grandma and mom were back in the living room. I could feel the silent tension. Everyone with their fingers crossed that it should work. It was too much of drama, I need a break, this should work out god, I prayed.

"I am really sorry about the delay; I had to avert a crisis. So sorry "he said. Wait a minute this voice was familiar. I would know this voice anywhere. I mean I just heard it a few hours ago.

I looked up and saw the same shock, mirror in the face of Vikram who walked in.

Chapter 5 - Tamarind

Vikram was looking down at the ground; I was seated opposite him in the back garden by the money plant. The sun was setting, and it looked as if the sky was on fire. The oranges and tinge of red, I must get a sari that colour I thought. Vikram cleared his throat. I turned around and looked at him. He put his head down again.

"I," he started.

"Vikram there are rats in our back garden and the baby mice run in the shrub over there," I said.

Vikram shot out of the chair, and Krish tumbled out of the shrub, where he was hiding. Vikram screamed in terror as he thought the large rat was landing from the shrub. My brothers, aunt, grandma were all out in a second and Krish was marched into the house.

"Vikram, my cousin Krish did that last time," I said. "I really don't think he is at an age where he should be listening to our conversation."

"I am sorry Santhoshi. I...I... I," Vikram said.

Vikram had told me his whole love story on the flight. He was a budding fashion designer, and he was in love with the tailor. Their team is the kind that dreams are made of. This guy was going to rock the ramps of Delhi and Bombay some day. Oh, did I forget to mention that Vikram's lover, John was pissed off that he was coming to the village suddenly? He was clueless that he was being brought to the Bride viewing. I can only imagine his plight when he saw me seated like a decorated Christmas tree.

34 *Spices Are Sweet*

He was late in arriving at our house, since he had been pacifying John.

John had enrolled Vikram for an important fashion competition. The finals were the day after and instead Vikram was here at my place being forced to eat Tiffin (teatime snack) at our house. I had promised to meet Vik and John, when I was in Bangalore next time. He promised to make me a rocking new dress.

"You can tell your parents you don't like me," I said.

"What's there not to like you? I like you as a great person. I mean you listened to my whole story without being shocked. I was so relieved talking to you," Vikram said.

"My parents will be heartbroken that this is not on. I don't know what to say. I won't say anything about you," I said.

"I will take care of it Santhoshi. Thank you so much "Vikram said.

He got up and made a gesture as if to hug me. I quickly moved away.

"The walls have ears and eyes Vikram, Good luck!"

We were back in the living room to the expectant faces of my relatives and his parents.

Aunt SM held my hand when she bid goodbye and said "You are the one my child."

I could not look at her face or Vikram's, I felt so sad. They seemed like nice people to have as in laws. Vikram as a fashion designer, wow I could have gone to all the fashion shows. This is so damn depressing. Everyone waved goodbye and went into the house.

"Thank God Ashok had a girl friend, we got a better proposal for our daughter," Mom said rubbing her hands in delight.

"Vikram is so good looking like Lord Krishna," grandma said. "I did not want to go close to him; he looked like a movie star."

"Did you see how they asked Santhoshi to sit as soon as she came," papa said.

"He is kind of cool sis, I am happy for you," Anish continued.

"I am tired, can I go to bed," I asked.

They quickly bid me good-bye, and I could hear my aunt ask about how much SMs were worth financially, as I went up.

I changed my clothes and switched on the mobile. Four missed calls from Maya, I was in no mood to listen to her tell me that I am a loser. I fell into an uneasy sleep where Vikram, and I were getting married, John rushes in to stop the marriage. Oh except John looked like the actor John A. I woke up in a sweat with all these good-looking men, running havoc in my dreams and all being gay. I mean what kind of nonsense is this. My mobile was blinking with a text message.

My parents believe only in the astrologer. He had said we matched perfectly in our star signs. I paid him handsomely to say that it was bad luck for you, if you marry me, to your parents. I am off to Bangalore, and I am sending you not one but two dresses to your friend Maya's place. Text message from Vikram.

I cheered up with the thought of my two new dresses. Seriously, it's not every day the man says no and you get two dresses thrown in freely. I changed into my track pants and decided to do yoga to clear my mind and work out the stress.

I jogged up to the terrace, as I did my *surya namaskar*; I watched the sunrise. I felt warm and glowing and full of life. Yoga gives you this blood rush and a sense of calmness that can be felt inside not explained completely, until you try it out yourself.

To escape the talk of the SM family I decided to visit my dad's sister in the next village. Grandma would accompany me. So off we set off on our little trip. I fell asleep as soon as I got into the car. We arrived two hours later. My aunt came running out in delight.

"Welcome, welcome. I am so happy that you decided on a spontaneous visit. I have cooked your favourite food for both of you. I have new jasmine flowers for Santhoshi's hair. I have bought glass bangles from the fair for her," she chattered.

We were served with *buttermilk* (a cooling drink made from yoghurt, salt and spices) to drink and *Muruku*, a flour-based

36 *Spices Are Sweet*

pretzel like snack, which is usually oily but my aunt makes it the best without oil. This aunt and uncle lived in a simple house. My uncle actually worked in the paddy fields, whereas the uncle's back home and papa have people to do all the work. Grandma went off to the neighbour's house to hear the stories of the village.

My aunt asked me about my parents, and spoke about the temple festival, when she would come to our village. Grandma came back with about ten women, from the neighbourhood, who she had brought over to show them her granddaughter. One of the women was carrying a cute two-year-old baby, who jumped into my arms, when I held out my hands. She smiled in delight. The women were all chattering about many different topics - from cooking, to the village, to temples, to the weather.

It was soon time for lunch. The *Tamarind* curry, mixed vegetable curry, potato fry and pickles were so tasty. My uncle walked in as we were finishing the lunch with a big Jackfruit from his garden. Jackfruits are prickly outer covered fruit with a sweet yellow flesh. The sweetness is sugary and tasty. Grandma was trying to eat one too many, and we had to take it away from her since she is diabetic.

The bliss of a big lunch can only be topped off with a nap. We therefore, took a good nap for an hour on the mat, which was put out on the floor. In the evening, after coffee and snacks again it was time to leave. My aunt filled my hands with mirror bangles. The gold, red and green made a colourful pattern. She adorned my hair with flowers and gave me more to take home to mom.

I was listening to the iPod on the way back, and grandma was asleep again. We reached home in the night and were welcomed by the cook who whispered that mom was ill and in bed. Anish and dad and the rest of the family was nowhere in sight. Grandma and I rushed to amma's room. Amma was lying down and staring at the ceiling. I touched her forehead, and she looked at me with so much pain in her eyes.

"The astrologer said it was not good for you if you marry Vikram. We wanted to do any prayer that could fix the bad omen, but he said there is nothing we could do," mom said and her eyes filled with tears.

"Vikram wants to marry your mom?" asked Grandma in shock.

I burst out laughing, trust grandma to come up with classic lines. Mom sat up in annoyance and explained the situation to grandma. I just sat there trying to control my laughter. Grandma was quick to dismiss the whole episode lightly.

"We will go see our astrologer Santhoshi, we will fix this immediately. The next time you get a proposal, you will get married," mom said with a final note.

"How is papa?" I asked her.

"You only care about your father's feelings. You did not even ask how I feel. Papa is fine, he is a man," mom replied.

"You are a woman, you should be able to control your feelings," grandma said.

They started arguing aimlessly, and I had to leave the room.

I thought I should return the missed calls from Maya, Karthik and Priya. They had all been calling me regularly, and I just did not reply to any of them. Maya had even gone to the extent of saying top urgent in her text message, which she had sent twenty times. I dialled her mobile. She picked up on the first ring.

"I hate you, I don't want to ever talk to you, you cow," she screamed.

"I am sorry, too many things happened when I reached home," I said.

"I called you from so many numbers. What were you doing? Taking the cows out for a bath?" she said. "Priya is getting married."

"Uh," I said.

"Yes she is getting married; her parents have seen someone for her from the states. Priya looked at the photo and said yes," Maya said. "The guy is in India on vacation and the wedding is in two weeks time!"

That is how fast, sometimes, Indian weddings get fixed. Priya's parents were hurriedly looking for a wedding hall to have the big Indian wedding.

Chapter 6 - Sandalwood

The following morning I heard the sudden pounding of my door. Opened it to find mom already decked up and ready to go.

"Good morning mom," I mumbled and headed off to my bed.

"Why are you not ready, I have fixed an appointment to see Mr. Astrologer?" she said.

I remembered hazily that she mentioned something about that last night, but did not expect her to rise and shine so early this morning. Quickly I showered and changed, and was whisked off to the astrologer, without breakfast. Mom wanted me to skip my breakfast ,as a mark of respect to get my stars read.

We were at the waiting room for two hours. I kept looking at the watch and at my mom with agitation, which was growing by the minute. The long wait was to see Mr. Astrologer.

Mr. Astrologer lived in the neighbouring village and was celebrated in the area. My parents consulted all significant decisions with him. My horoscope (astrological data) had already been run by him, written and ready for sale. Oops, ready in case anyone wanted to match it.

The system is such that my horoscope would be matched with a prospective groom's horoscope and the wedding would be fixed, if it gets a score of 60 percent or above. The planetary alignments are matched in strategic ways to find the match. So here we were in the waiting line to see him and to ask what was going to happen with me.

He had given us an appointment, but had someone else with him at that time, and we were waiting. It seemed like forever and my mother had finished gossiping about all our relatives, neighbours and friends.

Walking into his room, where he reads your chart, you are first hit with the number of framed photos of all the gods hanging in the room. All religions are in there in full glory. The smell of sandalwood incense and slight chanting from the CD are supposed to give an impression of being relaxed. I was not relaxed; it made me feel more edgy. I checked the astrologer out; he was a burly guy, who reminded me of our cousin, whom we don't talk to anymore. He was wearing so many rings on his fingers, and a large gold chain with a god pendant on it.

He closed his eyes and went into a trance and said "I can feel it; you are here without a belief that I can help you".

My mom, being subtle is her the middle name, nudged me hard. She was certainly getting high on this bit of information. There was a growling sound. Oh, god actually this man has a tiger or lion hidden under his table. Astrologer, mom and I looked around in confusion. The growl was extremely clear; it was my poor stomach on strike that it was empty.

"Well, let us read your chart," he said, completely ignoring the fact that I was starving.

Then he went onto a monotone and explained that I need to change the spelling of my name and be wary of strangers. Stranger danger is an immense problem in my life, so I was asked to come back to do some prayers to fix it and make it right. My mom was overjoyed since this involved coming back here again.

Mom said, "Swami I have a very important question to you, my daughter has lost her mobile, and we want to know who would have taken it?"

I looked at mom since I don't see this guy having some tracking system to track down my lost mobile. By the way, the mobile was lost a few months ago when I was at a wedding. Therefore, the whole point of this issue was lost in translation there.

Mr. A looked slightly bemused by my mom's so called intelligent question and did the next best thing. He ignored her question

40 Spices Are Sweet

about the lost mobile and went on looking at my chart. He then said I had to add the letters H to my name, and it will bring me a home, hope, happiness, harmony and health. Very importantly, it will bring me the elusive husband.

"We will replace all the certificates and everything," Mom said.

The astrologer and I looked in doubt. Then like a ping, it dropped on my poor head, which was hurting with hunger. She wanted to change everything with an H.

"She wants to make a spelling change on my certificate," I said.

"Not necessary at all, you can just sign your name in this new spelling. Also, write it out with the new spelling a hundred times," said astrologer with a big smile.

Mom jumped up in delight as if I was already wedded. She paid him a considerable amount, and we were on our way.

"It's done my child I feel so much at ease," mom said.

"My stomach wants some peace mom, can I have a piece of sweet or something," I asked her.

Mom smiled happily and took me to the temple. In the temple, she bought me *Prasad* (food offerings given to god). I ate it slowly savouring the spice of the tamarind rice and the sourness of the curd rice. Mom had rushed off to pray some more.

I sat out felt the breeze on my face. The massive stone structure and the strength of its architecture, never fail to amaze me. Black and grey stones used up so many hundreds of years ago to create such a monumental structure. I watched the tourists' line up to take pictures, and the worshippers walk in with flowers as offerings. The shops, which were lined outside, sold little trinkets of bangles, *bindis* (little dot and design stickers for your forehead), incense and the latest prayer CDs.

I was busy browsing the shops and bargaining with the guys in the shop. The shopkeeper was humouring me by refusing my bargaining. I think bargaining is a tradition that I have picked up from the women in the family, and I feel the need to use it.

Mom rushes out and scolds me for not going in to pray. I rush into the temple; I feel the peace and coolness. Quickly recited my prayers and a look around the temple (a full circle around the whole temple completes the prayer).

That night Priya's parents the Shahs had called dad, to get permission for me to come for ten days to their house in the village, for the wedding. Papa was not happy, but had agreed to send me ahead. My mom and dad would come for the wedding and bring me back with them. We had to quickly sort out air tickets for me to go to Hyderabad. I planned the logistics with Maya so that we could meet at the airport.

I felt ecstatic at the little trip. I was unable to get through to Priya, whenever I called her. Priya was at the beautician, she was at the cloth store, jewellery shop and visitors. I got these responses from her assisting family members. I looked forward to this trip.

42 *Spices Are Sweet*

Chapter 7 - Masala Chai

I arrived at Hyderabad Airport. My flight was uneventful with an old lecherous uncle trying to talk to me and me ignoring him. No more good-looking gay guys as travel companions. I pushed my trolley piled high with luggage (it was ten days I had to pack in case of emergency) to meet Maya. She had arrived at the airport, one hour earlier from Bangalore and planned to fill me up and for us to travel to Priya's Village.

I rushed to hug Maya who did not hug me back. She had a look of surprise on her face.

"Babes you have put on so much weight," Maya says.

"No I haven't," I said, and boy was I annoyed.

"Yes you have, what is this?" She said pinching my midriff. "Have you been eating fried food with your grandma, just sitting by to watch the village go and eat kachoris all day, stuffing your mouth with your grandma, this is disgusting. It has been only a few weeks since I last saw you."

I rushed off with a huff and pushed the trolley. I mean this whole bride viewing and mom moping had been a bit frustrating for me. "Bang," I had knocked my trolley with a ferocious looking Aunt's trolley. She started screaming and shouting at me that I was stupid. I wanted to cry, was I having PMS?

"The fat cells have taken over your mind Santhoshi," Maya said.

I turned and looked at her and burst out laughing. We were laughing so hard, that the screaming aunt got angrier and shouted at the cops to arrest us. We continued our laughter and kept moving.

DD 43

Maybe I should lower my snacking with grandma at home. Then again, Yoga has been also quite nonexistent in practice. Grandma and I had been eating all the fried food we could put our hands on, and our mouth was like a non-stop food processor the past weeks. I thought I was doing her a favour by accompanying her, but now I realise I must be having a whopping depression.

"Maya I have been depressed," I said. "Oh my god all this stress and my life being a disorder."

Maya shot her eyebrows up "Yup that's about right," she said and walked off.

We saw guys jumping up and down, with the board Welcome to The Shahs Wedding. There were about seven boards. People were approaching the boards at a speed. We immediately rushed to a man who took out a list of about 200 names. The expected arrival at the domestic airport was 200 for the big fat Indian wedding. We got into the allocated car.

"How long is the drive?" Maya asked in Telugu (the local language.)

"Two hours madam," He said.

"Can we stop and eat I am hungry?" I asked.

Maya turned and looked at me "Missing a couple of meals might do you some good, if you want to look half decent at the wedding."

"Shut up," I said to her.

My phone rings distracting my anger.

"Have you reached there? I miss you, I am eating some nice *bajis* (onion rings) and missed you," grandma screams into the mobile.

Maya bursts out laughing. I quickly cut my conversation with grandma short.

"You are making stuff up Santhoshi; your depression is not related to your eating, because you are stuffing your face out of boredom. You know that, I know that. You have to stop this man search and tell your parents that you want to study," Maya

44 *Spices Are Sweet*

said. "You are intelligent and beautiful and bound to find a nice guy. It will happen at the time it is meant to."

"You are boring me just shut up," I said.

"Let's have some *masala chai* (tea with spices)," she said.

I smiled at her.

"Oh dear your face just lit up when I mentioned a tea," she shakes her head.

I punched her and off we were to Priya's place. We arrived at Priya's house in the afternoon. Her village house was a beehive of activity, with people walking in and out and painters finishing the painting work.

"Welcome my dears," shouted aunt Shah. "Priya's best friends" she said to a gang of women who were accompanying her. We all took a moment to do our head nodding. We walked into Priya's room, filled with her young cousins.

Priya was wearing a beautiful cream and red sari and looked fantastic. There is a saying that when a woman is ready to get married, she gets a natural glow which all the facials in the world cannot buy. I could see that in Priya's face, and it was glowing with happiness. She rushed to hug us both and broke into excited chatter, introducing the cousin clan.

My head was confused with all the names and what each one of them was doing. We smiled and nodded.

"Shall I show you your room?" Priya said.

"Yes," I started and was cut short by Maya.

"We are staying with you in this room. We can get a mat on the floor. I want to spend each moment possible before the wedding with you," Maya said.

"Priya will need lots of beauty sleep before the wedding and the big night. You should not bother her," interrupts Priya's cousin Sheetal.

"Maybe you guys should leave her alone for her to rest," retorts Maya.

DD 45

Oh oh thinks my poor brain. Now do we have to come and pick a fight at the wedding even before it started?

"You guys can all stay here with me, we can all spend time together," says Priya who has missed the disturbing note in Mayas voice.

Maya strides purposefully out of the room. I am just left there, with a bunch of luggage around my feet. Priya looks confused, and her cousins look pissed.

Priya laughs nervously, and looks at me and says, "I like the way you look, chubby and well fed, and it suits you".

"Mhem," I say.

If she was trying to compliment me let's just say that she had missed the point. God I was fat. Maya is back with Priya's mom. Oh, hell what has she done now?

"Priya baby, what happened to your eyes, you got eye bags under your eyes," Aunt Shah rushes and holds her face.

What the hell, what bags? I look on with no idea as Maya points to Priya's flawless face and makes noises of concern.

"Ok everyone out of the room. Priya will rest a bit and let Santhoshi and Maya stay here and take care of her, as you obviously haven't," aunt screams." How much am I suppose to handle? Now her friends will do it since you are just not doing anything properly."

"But," starts two of Priya's cousins, but are shut up by a bombard of Telugu from aunt. I look at Maya, who winks back at me.

Aunt and the cousins who stare at us with hatred make their way out of the room. It is three of us alone. Priya looks extremely nervous and peers into the mirror.

"Mirror Mirror on the wall who is the prettiest of the Shahs," Maya says.

I recover quickly from ignorance and the brain works "They all look like Cinderella's step sisters says mirror!"

Maya and I burst out laughing as Priya shouts, "I hate you cows!" and comes to hit us.

46 *Spices Are Sweet*

"You told aunt that Priya's got bags under her eyes, and she bought it?" I ask Maya who nods and checks her makeup.

"I want my cousins to be here with us as well," whines Priya.

"Just shut up, they are always hovering around, we hardly speak these days. You are going to get married and go away, spend the last few days with us. We are in for dinner with Karthik in Hyderabad tonight," Maya says.

"We can't go out, my whole family is here," says Priya.

"Where are we going for dinner?" I ask simultaneously.

"We are going out and having fun without your blooming cousins. I told your mom that I am taking you for a special face thing. So just shut it," says Maya.

The rest of the conversation is interrupted by a knock at the door. I open it to find two helpers carrying an extra bed. They bring it in and place it near Priya's and leave the room.

"When did Karthik come to Hyderabad?" I ask.

"I made him come down for the night, he was ever so reluctant. So I told him that Santhoshi is running away with a man, and we have to stop her," Maya says.

"What the hell. Why did you have to drag my name? You could have run away, or Priya could have, Why me?" I scream.

Knock knock. I find Sheetal on the door, "So, you are running away is it. Wait till I tell aunt." she snorts.

Oh, brilliant, now I am running away with an imaginary man and getting threatened by Priya's cousin all at the same moment. Maya pulls Sheetal in and signals me to lock the door.

"Leave me alone, don't touch me," shouts Sheetal pushing Maya. Priya runs up quickly to break the little tussle.

"Can we get the brain cells working here, please?" asks Maya.

Obviously, that has to be me. "Sheetal have you felt love the way Romeo and Juliet have," I ask Sheetal.

"No and I am not interested," says Sheetal.

DD 47

"Why is it that do you like girls then," I ask her.

Sheetal looks flummoxed for a moment. Oh, my god the woman is still trying to figure out what she likes.

"I know what you are going through Sheetal, and let me tell you that I am going to sort out your problem before I run away." I say. I hold my heart idiotically and try to look like in love except I see Maya trying hard not to laugh and Priya looking decidedly worried. Sheetal looked more confused than ever before and shakes her head slowly. I nod my head like a Jack in the Box. Oh, god my head is going to fall off at this rate. Sheetal leaves the room in confusion.

Chapter 8 - Mint

We were seated at Hyderabad's China doll Restaurant. The Chinese decor and the pleasing waiting staff was a welcome. Oh, I think the *mojito* cocktails, we had consumed might have been helping me see things in a different light. We were all dressed up and happily, where we had to be. Priya was on the phone with her Man Ajay like five times since we had arrived. Oh well, we were waiting for Karthik who was unusually late. Maya had been on the phone with him on our way, after we got here and let's say she was edgy. I was pleasantly seeing things in a happier note. I mean Priya is getting married, how exciting it is. Sheetal thinks I am running away with a Romeo of the new age, how exciting. Oh damn it; I am drunk after three cocktails. This is what happens when you live in a village and take alcohol in small doses, which are really imaginary.

"I have had enough," says Maya pulling Priya's mobile away and snapping me back in action.

"You guys are so bloody boring!" she continues.

"But Maya you are so pushy, I want to talk to Ajay," Priya says.

I nod enigmatically, I mean Priya should continue her conversation, and I should go back to moping around and staring at the mint leaves in my drink.

"Santhoshi wake up you idiot," Maya says. "Let's play truth or dare."

Priya and I look at each other we don't want to do anything. She wants to go back to her phone, and I want to go back to dreaming.

"Truth or dare," shouts Maya.

"Truth," Priya says.

"Do you really like this marriage?" asks Maya.

Priya silently stares back at Maya. I look at the two of them. Where does Maya come up with these questions?

"She is happy, of course she is," I answer.

"Shut up," says Maya.

"I am very happy Maya. I think you should stop questioning everything and live life a little. I am so darned sure I like this," Priya says.

"Good for you," says Maya sipping her drink and smiling into it.

"Truth or dare," I start up.

"Dare," says Maya.

I look at the cute waiter who has been smiling at me nonstop since I got here.

"Pinch his butt or tell me the truth," I say spontaneously. Pinch a waiter's butt god where do I get these ideas. Priya and Maya burst out laughing. She signals the waiter. Holy cow what is she going to do now; I hold my breath and look at Priya who looks as flummoxed as me. Maya bends on the menu and asks him a question, and I see her hand reach out and pinch his butt. Oh my god. I look at Priya; she looks petrified. The waiter, oh dear the poor man he looked shocked, surprised and utterly horrified. He stammers something and rushes off.

"You stupid cow, we are going to get arrested," I blurt.

"Well it was your dare!" says Maya smiling.

"If my fiancé knows this he might stop the wedding," whines Priya.

"If he would stop the wedding because of my dare. Don't you think you should rethink about if you really want this marriage?" asks Maya.

"Hey sorry I am late," says Karthik.

We turn around to see Karthik who has just walked in. He looks the same gorgeous as ever, but his beautiful brown eyes look much stressed. Wait did I say gorgeous and brown eyes

50 *Spices Are Sweet*

about my friend; I am obviously out of sorts. He hugs Maya and Priya.

He turns towards me saying, "Wow you have put on weight, and you look so lovely, it suits you," and hugs me tight.

Is it my imagination or did he just hold me a bit too long. My weight gain is the source of every conversation. I look at Priya and Maya, Maya does the one eyebrow thing. (What's up? You ask with your eyebrows arched.)

His mobile rings insistently and he picks it up and looks more stressed answering, "Yes, I just got here. Santhoshi, Maya and Priya are here. Yes, Santhoshi got permission to come for dinner. Yes!"

I got permission did I, well I don't remember calling and asking for permission.

"It's rude to carry on the phone when the ladies are waiting," says Maya.

"I'll call you back," Karthik hangs up.

"Vidya, she wanted to know how you guys were. She always asks about you," he continued looking at me.

"How would you know how we were, you never pick up our calls," says Maya.

"I am so sorry, the work, wedding and all this new stuff. How are you all?" He says looking around.

"Pinching a waiter's butt and running off with an imaginary man and panting to get married, I think we are doing good Karthik," I say.

Priya and Maya burst out laughing, and Karthik just looks around. We update him, and he gets a drink and starts to relax, but is interrupted by his mobile buzzing with texts nonstop. He keeps saying its Vidya. It was obvious that she was not giving him sweet endearments, but probably was questioning on what we were up to. Did I mention that Vidya had ogle eyes? Yeah I think we covered that. Karthik excuses himself to the washroom with his mobile, probably to call his ladylove.

"Oh dear what's with the man?" asks Priya.

"Same virus which bit you Priya!" I say.

"I think Karthik should have married one of us," says Maya.

Priya and I turn and to look at her in wonderment. Maya nods her head, biting into the spicy chicken wing.

"I did have a crush on him," says Priya. Now we turn and look at her.

"What the hell, I did too," said Maya.

Then they turn and look at me. Oh dear did I have a crush on him too? I mean I can't think of anything profound to say.

"Ya she did, Santhoshi makes the googly eye thing with him," says Maya.

"What I don't ok. I used to ponder it would have saved a lot of trouble if he married me, I mean we are the same caste," I say.

Then the three of us look at each other and burst out laughing.

"Seriously, looking at him now I don't think so," says Maya.

"Ya he is so stressed," says Priya.

"I want to see Vidya at the wedding," I say.

Karthik comes back, looking more stressed than ever and just sits there moping into his plate of food. I look at him, I feel sad for him. Then for a moment, I wonder am I going to be in the same place, when I am engaged. Our dinner is unusually quiet, as each of us is lost in his, hers thoughts and when we hug goodbye to him, I am glad that the whole thing is over.

"Will see you at the wedding Karthik," Priya says.

"I am sorry Priya, I made it today, because I won't be able to come for the wedding. We are off to Vidya's uncle's temple for a special *pooja* on your wedding date." He says.

"What?" Priya sulks.

"Are you serious?" I ask.

Maya does not say anything; she just turns her face. Karthik goes on to explain, how he has to go do this *pooja* on that particular day. He does not look attractive to me anymore. Our travel back to Priya's is still with each of us, lost in our innermost thoughts.

52 *Spices Are Sweet*

Chapter 9 - Camphor

The next morning we are seated in front of the breakfast plates piled high with yummy food. Sheetal stares at us in hatred and her cousins also look at us in disapproval. Aunt Shah is very pleased with Priya's looks, she thinks she is glowing six times more and asks Maya for the contact details. Maya looks a little lost, when I step in and save her, by telling aunt, we should guard the beauty secret, or all the cousins will be lining there for appointments. Aunt and Maya look pleased with my explanation. I look over at Priya whispering on her mobile phone, looking ever so pleased. The secret was simple it was called first love.

We are taken to the temple to do special prayers before the wedding. Seated in front of the lamp and praying, I ask dear God show me the path and help me out. I want to get married too; I stare at the Marigold flower in front of me as if it had the answer for me. The hour long special prayer session is filled with all the women in the family. The married ones praying for husbands, the unmarried seeking for a husband. I reach out to touch the camphor lit plate, which is burning brightly like a firecracker. A piece drops in front of me.

"Good Luck for the bride and for this girl," announces an old aunt.

"Yes!" Shouts aunt and comes excitedly towards the fire piece.

Priya looks thrilled and Maya rolls her eyes. I just look at the little fireball crackle in front of me. After all this, I need some sort of good luck for my next bride viewing, I pray wholeheartedly to god. My parents have been on the phone asking, if I was ok and how much grandma missed me. I missed home too, although I was very bored there. We were at the roof terrace watching the kids, send out kites into the clear blue sky.

We were to go with the women to buy some more clothes for the relatives in the afternoon. Indian weddings involve new clothes for most of the relatives and friends. Aunt had a room full of saris labelled with names and the price tag hanging in there. Priya's Trousseau was full of beautiful saris, and *churidhars*. We teased about how she is going to wear all this and run around in New York. Priya had so much of luggage with her casual clothes and all this beautiful Indian clothes as well.

After another, a huge meal of rice and curry we were asked to rest and get ready to go shopping. What bliss to eat and rest, I love the afternoon nap after a full meal. We were off in a big van with the cousins and aunts to the clothes shop. It would be only the chosen lucky shop that the Shahs had been shopping for years now.

We were warmly welcomed by the shop Manager. I mean we looked like the Big Indian Wedding shoppers. When so many women walk in a group and most with their beautiful silk saris and the shiny gold jewellery, it is a shop owners dream come true. We were taken into the silk sari section, where the women started pulling the whole display case apart, pointing at a hundred saris at the same time.

"So did you speak to him?" I hear a whisper and turn to see Sheetal standing next to me.

"Who?" I ask.

"You know who!" she says.

What the hell is on with this girl? We are interrupted by Priya's cute two-year-old niece who runs up to me and puts her two chubby hands out to be carried. So I carry her into my arms and she smiles at me happily.

Maya looks out with a bored look and Priya is surrounded by her cousins looking at even more Indian clothes that she will not need. Sheetal is just hovering around me. We are served hot coffee and sweets by the shop owner. I drink the coffee and stroll up to Maya.

"What's with the sulky face?" I ask.

"I don't know why you are so happy and cheery all the time." She says with a sigh.

54 *Spices Are Sweet*

"Well it would help to put a cheery face and not sulk like Cinderella's step sister," I reply back.

"Everything is changing; you guys hardly pick up the mobiles. Priya is so distracted by the wedding and you are just waiting to be hitched. It's like we are pushed into adulthood so soon," Maya says.

"You left out Karthik who has got a severe case of hen peckedness," I say.

Maya laughs out loud and I join her.

"Yes you are right, I am happy that none of us did end up with him, He is so scared of that woman. Not coming to Priya's wedding is so unforgivable." She continues.

"Yes, I think it's all for the best," I say.

"What are you girls gossiping about?" Priya comes from behind us.

"Well how you have become like the aunts and obsessed with your wedding," I say.

"Noooo," she shouts.

"Just kidding, let's go look at more lovely saris that you don't need," I say.

"Ajay's family is coming this evening to discuss the wedding rituals with my parents and you can meet him at last," Blushes Priya.

"At last we meet the man who stole our friend from us," says Maya.

Aunt Shah and the rest of the aunt gang, cousins come with about five boys, carrying about ten bags or more of the purchases. They look a happy bunch. Oh maybe except for Sheetal, who looks like a dark cloud has settled on her head. I need to talk to that girl later.

Its night, when we get home and there is a flurry of activity for the grooms' family arrival. Aunt Shah is giving instructions about dinner and what to serve. The cousins are running to do their makeup. So is Priya, who is showering and re-doing her makeup and changing her clothes. Maya and I get ready as well.

"They have come!" shouts a cousin.

Priya does the blushing thing again, looks down demurely and walks out slowly. Maya rolls her eyes at me. I giggle and follow her out. We come to the massive living room area, with its many couches, taken up with loads of adults.

Ajay stands out in the crowd. It's pretty obvious it's him with his Abercrombie T-shirt and Levis jeans. He smiles at Priya and she smiles back so happily. He nods his head at me and Maya. He looks so suited to Priya is what runs in my mind. The adults are happily talking away about the rituals and how they should keep with time. All the men nod their heads in agreement.

"We get late, only when the women go to get dressed and do make up," booms an uncle.

Everyone laughs at this heartily. Aunt Shah looks so happy and reminds me of mom. The groom's family consisting of about six members are taken to the dining room to have dinner. Priya is asked to join them and she refuses politely telling them she will have dinner with her friends and cousins later.

"So what do u think?" asks Priya.

"He seems nice," I say.

"Very happy for you," Maya says hugging her.

Chapter 10 - Banana Leaf

Seven days later, we are at the *Big Indian Wedding*. The Hindu customs of a wedding are slightly different differing from community to community and caste to caste . The community and caste involves about 100, with another hundreds of different sections. The necessary rituals consist of the engagement, making of the *Thali* (a religious chain with pendants symbolising gods), the wedding day where you tie the Thali to the bride and a reception.

We were at the beautifully decorated wedding hall, consisting of two thousand or more invitees.

Break down as follows:

250 Immediate relatives.

100 Indirect relatives (aunts-in-laws, sister's pet parrot, cousin later removed.)

100 relatives by marriage (cousin got married and her in laws brothers cousins family.)

1000 community members (you belong to a community you invite them although you probably know only 50 per cent of them.)

50 bride's and groom's friends (they would have invited a hundred each from school days to college days, only fifty turn up.)

The rest are people consisting of a list of neighbours-old and new, friends old and new and their kids and their in-laws, and a significant number of people that you actually don't know.

The beautiful ceremony is colourful. The ladies are in the brightest of reds, blues, greens, oranges saris, and an array of diamond, ruby, sapphire and gold jewellery. The men in their bright white or beige silk shirts and *dhotis* (a skirt like long attire) or their Indian pants (lose fitting pants).

The flowers used in decoration and the garlands which adorn the bride and groom are reds, oranges and green leaves. The wedding ceremony starts with religious chanting and the tying of the *Thali* with three knots.

My parents and Maya's parents are engaged in conversation from the time they came to the wedding. Our dads are probably discussing the world economic position and government. Moms, oh well, they must be gossiping about us.

Maya and I stay with Priya until she gets dressed and goes to the ceremony. We hug her goodbye before the ceremony because we probably won't get a word edgewise when there are a thousand people waiting to greet her. We were both leaving with our parents in the evening.

Our gift to Priya was a framed photograph of, yes you guessed it right, us. I know it's a bit cheesy, but I came up with the bright idea. So we had got a photo of the three of us in the first year of college and framed it and given it to her. We had spoken to Ajay a couple of times on the mobile; he seemed polite and was kind enough to invite us to America. They were leaving in the next few days. It seemed so far away.

We were at the wedding lunch, and I was counting the number of dishes they were serving. I always do this at the weddings. It was set out on a large banana leaf and consisted of 30 dishes inclusive of three different sweets and desserts.

As we were leaving, I noticed mom with an upset face. It was sudden after lunch. Oh dear, poor mom is jealous I thought. My friends got married, and I am still in the market. I must cheer her up; I should start adding the H and write my name to please her.

We say goodbyes and thank aunt and uncle Shah for their charming and generous hospitality. Maya and I had got beautiful blue silk saris for the wedding. I asked Maya to visit me in the village; I can't expect my parents to let me run around the country again after all this.

58 *Spices Are Sweet*

So we are back at the airport. I did ask mom if she is OK on our way to the airport, she just looked tenser than ever. Papa meets a friend and walks off to have a coffee with him. I hear soft crying. I turn around and see mom crying into her handkerchief.

"Uhm mom get over it," I say. I mean seriously she can't be so blatantly jealous of Priya.

"How can I get over it? My child, my child," mom says.

"Mom the time has to come," I say. Seriously, how can my wedding happen without the right planetary alignments?

"Your father is going to kill me," she says.

"What is mom talking about? Oh well sure, we do find out.

"I told you how important it is to marry someone in our community. Nobody in our whole family has ever run away," mom says.

"Yes I know that, who is running away?" I ask.

"You are planning to run away and ask me, I know it's hard to live with someone else when your heart is elsewhere," mom continues to cry so dramatically.

I quickly do a check. Dad's a bit far off but we have caught the attention of fellow passengers.

Shit.

"Mom what are you talking about," I ask her.

"You. How much your poor mother has suffered for you?" mom says, while catching her breath. " Sheetal told me."

"Oh god mom, Sheetal is lying," I say; I am going to kill that woman when I meet her next. "Where did you meet her?"

"She came up to me, when I was washing my hand. She said you are running away with Romeo. Who is Romeo? He is not our caste or our religion. Papa will be heartbroken. Grandma will have a heart attack, and your poor mom will just drop dead," she says with a tearful woe.

"We bring up our kids with so much of care and responsibility and look at what they do," says some woman sitting next to mom.

DD 59

"Mom stop it, Sheetal is lying. There is nobody, I told her a Shakespeare story of Romeo and Juliet," I say clearly, shaking mom.

Oh dear, I see dad looking this way. I just wave back and smile like an idiot at him. He nods his head and looks as if he is finishing his tea to come here.

"Mom, Sheetal is a girl, who likes girls and she likes me. That's why she lied to you?" I say. Where do I come up with this sort of thing?

"What?" Mom asks, her tears stopping, immediately.

"WHAT?" Shouts the passenger, who has been eavesdropping.

"Oh Krishna, I don't want to hear this kind of awful thing," mom says, closing her ears.

"Continue your story," says nosy Parker excitedly.

"I am going to tell Papa!" I say.

"No don't tell him anything, Papa might get sick if he hears this. We should not have sent you to the wedding. I won't send you anywhere my child. It's a big bad world," says mom.

I smile at her, and yes, it is a big bad world indeed. I am little red riding hood, Sheetal's the vicious wolf.

"So what else is the story?" asks nosy parker with a grin.

"Get lost you stupid woman, were you this nosy in your house? Go poke your nose somewhere else," says mom to nosy parker.

Mom rushes off to wash her face, I quickly change seats and can feel inquisitive staring at me. Papa strides back and smiles at me.

"What were you and *amma* doing?" he asked.

"Nothing papa, we do this new yoga while sitting," I say.

"You shouldn't do all this and attract attention in public Santhoshi. It's entirely that woman and your mothers fault. She does not know what she is doing half the time," he says shaking his head.

60 *Spices Are Sweet*

"I have to tell you something, we thought of fixing you up with Raj. You know Raj, Nandini's brother in law!" Papa says.

I feel numb; I look at him with my mouth open.

"He has changed his ways," papa continues. "You will be close to the village, and you can visit us."

Mom comes back and sits.

"I have some fantastic news Santhoshi," she says smiling at me.

I have never felt this about my parents, in all of my twenty-five years of life, I hated them at that moment and wanted to burst out crying.

Chapter 11 - Chilli

We arrive at home, to find the house is in darkness.

"What is this not a single light is on or anything," says mum.

"*Amma Amma*,"calls out dad.

I just follow them in. I have not spoken a word, since hearing the happy news that they were going to screw up my life. I do agree with arranged marriages, I believe it works. The divorce rate is less, except a few hitches like Nandini, my sister's wedding. Nandini's marriage has been a financial burden to my parents. She was still spending off them. Nandini's husband Suresh is in a decent job and his family is well to do. She does not need to turn up randomly and create attention to my parents, but she does it because she is my evil sister. Nandini turns up frequently, and every time she comes, she has new set of demands. She is my greedy and evil sister.

Suresh's brother, Raj, the lecherous guy is a village rowdy. He is unemployed, lecherous and looks scary. If you look at his face, you will be distracted by a humongous black mole, which is near his nose, and actually, you cannot help but become fascinated by this distraction. I have not had conversations with Raj, but I must say he is not a person who gives up. Many a moment you can see him trying to make conversation or wink at me and go scratch scratch. Ugh, I feel like throwing up.

I am disturbed by my stream of thoughts when I realise there is a serious war inside the house.

"Well I don't want to light the lamp, switch on the lights or do anything," shouts grandma.

"Grandma, I missed you" I speed up to her. I did miss the old dear.

62 *Spices Are Sweet*

"You should have run off my child," says grandma, turning her face the other way.

Wait a minute did she just tell me something or is my hearing going, as well.

"Oh *amma* don't spoil the Childs head," says papa, switching on the lights.

My mom is in the prayer room, lighting lamps and getting on with the evening prayers, which have obviously not been performed.

"Run away Santhoshi, Krishna will take care of you," grandma rants. Krishna is not another person in the story, but our dear lord.

I was getting a headache. These past few days have been full of things I don't get, or I am thoroughly missing something.

"It's better she runs away than marry that no good loser" says grandma.

Oh, right so we are on the right track, there is someone who is on my side. My brother walks into the house he looks at me; he shakes his head in a sad and critical manner. I can understand his sign language, so there are few souls, who do not like this. Maybe they will help me avoid this crisis.

"No, Raj will change his ways and be good. Santhoshi will be so happy, and Nandini and she can live happily in the same house" mom says. I wonder if mum lives in delusion. She slows down at the last moment and looks pensive. I mean it was not like my sister and I are bosom buddies when she was here, so I have no clue why my mom thinks this is all going to change now.

"You messed up one daughter's life Latha, now you won't stop until you finish of this girl," shouts grandma.

"Stop all this noise!" screams my dad and he look frightfully angry.

I shoot up into my room and fall onto the bed. I feel depressed and dejected. Ugh, I think of Raj's mole and this horrible way he leerily says "hi".

I am sure he is up to no good and must be having many a mistress in every village up to the town. I burst out crying and I weep my heart out. You see we were taught to say yes only to arranged marriages but never taught to say no. I never foresaw that, in the future, my perfect arranged marriage would turn into a circus. I prayed so much for the perfect life without fail. Ok, maybe not perfect and least something with a little sanity.

Come to think of it, the past few weeks have been too much of a pressure. I realised maybe I don't need to get into this marriage act now. I have stopped doing yoga, being healthy, eating junk and doing nothing encouraging other than being obsessed about marriage. There is nothing wrong with me, it's just that I am not ready like all the others in my family are.

I get a text message from Maya that she has gone home and that she is bored and misses me. I just delete it; I am not in a mood to answer or update my plight which I have been faced with.

There is a small knock on my door, and I play deaf and don't reply. I feel the door open and look up in anger to see grandma walk in.

"Whole family has gone mad," she says. "You must not cry my child, we will stop this arrangement even before it starts".

"How do we stop a natural disaster, when it's going to happen? Why grandma?"

"Well the reason is your aunt was here five days back and told your mother that such bad luck that the bride viewing keeps getting messed up. Bad luck, bad luck, she repeated."

"OH!"

"Yes, your mother is a fool. She was crying and sobbing, and Nandini had phoned her. Your mother had told this to her, so she had suggested and convinced that it was meant to be that -Raj and you. Nandini also said that the family name should be kept without tarnishing and to save the third rejection. Nandini lives in a fool's world and would never wish you well. You think this old woman cannot hear. I can hear the things that I should hear. We still have the astrological match to do, I will arrange something there," my grandma says.

I looked at my grandma's wrinkled face. It was a face, which

64 *Spices Are Sweet*

had been through many ages. I took her hands into mine and saw the hard work it must have done in the days before. I don't remember my grandfather, since I was four, when he died of a heart attack. This magnificent woman in front of me had lived the last seventeen years alone. She only had memories of a man whom she lived with. She had the courage to stand up for me, and I was here bawling like a baby. Something in my head snapped.

I got up and washed my face. I came out, wiped my face with a towel and brushed my hair. Grandma was taking a short nap on my bed. I woke her up and told we will go down for dinner.

I walked into the dining room; my mom bustled out of the kitchen and called my brother and father for dinner. I sat down; I could feel mom watching me and nodding her head and making 'sign conversations' with my dad. My dad just looked on blankly. My grandma was staring at my mom, if looks could kill, mom would be dead meat. My brother was expressionless.

"Papa was I ever a burden to you," I ask.

There is silence at the table. Everyone's watching me with their mouths open, even the cook, and the maid is loitering at the doorway.

"Have I been a burden to you?" I ask loudly.

"No" Papa answers and looks at me.

I look straight into my dad's eyes.

"I will become a financial and mental burden, if you even think of discussing this alliance. I think the family had enough headaches dealing with Nandini's dramas. I would end up being a lifelong liability for you. I wouldn't be happy, you wouldn't be happy. I have always honoured your words and our culture, and I will marry the person you choose. I cannot accept someone who is not suitable for me, more importantly, who does not deserve to be your son-in-law," I say.

Phew that was the longest I have spoken to my dad in recent years. The silence is unbearable I watch my dad and cannot imagine what he is thinking.

"Can I have a *dosai* (spicy Indian pancake) *amma*?" I ask.

Mom's just standing there gaping at me and my dad.

"I am sorry Santhoshi, extremely sorry," papa says.

"I knew this was not meant to be, what terrific news," mom says.

"Latha I don't want you to utter a word anymore about this," papa says, and he smiles at me.

"How did you talk like that?" grandma asks.

"Magic in your hands grandma" I say smiling, and I know I am going to be OK.

66 *Spices Are Sweet*

Chapter 12 - Rice - Porridge

I was up the next day bright and early. Looking out of the window, I could see the birds chirping and the sun shining, it was such an ideal day. Suddenly, I could hear a loud voice yelling and screaming. I could hear someone running up the stairs and bang, bang. The door looked, as if it would be broken down, with the thudding.

I opened the door, to find an evil witch outside the door, my sister Nandini looked ready to beat me up and eat me alive.

"Who do you think you are? Some sort of *Maharani* (princess) to refuse a good proposal?" she yelled.

I looked at her and did not answer; I mean what kind of reply am I suppose to come up with. She was not a woman who would take silence for an answer; instead, she was a woman who could scream loudly.

"You have missed two proposals, already my relatives are saying that maybe you are cursed. I wanted to save you from the third proposal, which would have been a no. Don't you think that you should keep your status?" she yelled.

"You have not even bathed or gotten ready, its seven o clock. Papa and *amma* are stupid, they have spoilt you rotten!" she continued. "How can you just stand there and stare like a moron?"

"ENOUGH NANDINI," bellowed my dad from downstairs.

Grandma has appeared behind Nandini out of nowhere. "Papa told you to come down Nandini," she said smiling.

"Yes you keep petting her too grandma, you are partly to blame for all this. You were stirring unrest in the house from the day I brought this up. Why don't you behave your age and put some sense into her?" she yelled going downstairs.

"You better learn some manners," grandma shouted back.

"Get ready, we are going to visit my friend Lila, who is seriously ill and in her last moments," grandma said casually.

Lila, my grandma's childhood friend, was an old grandma, who lived about two roads away. Come to think I have not been to see her for a long time. She used to make the best *payasam* (rice porridge dessert) in our town. Ok, I should stop associating food with people and memories.

I remembered Nandini's words that I was cursed. I could not understand what I had done to her for her ever-harsh words. I came downstairs to find Nandini and mom talking to each other. . Grandma and I sat down and ate our breakfast of *dosai* and *chutney*. There was no move by either of them to join us or offer any words.

"We are going to see Lila," grandma said.

"Now don't take Santhoshi there, everyone is talking about her," mom said defiantly, without looking at me.

"Yes they are talking about what a lucky escape she had from marrying into that family. She is coming with me," grandma said and beckoned me to join her.

Seriously, mom was confused on whose side she was. We set out walking and grandma started on her story of how she and Grandma Lila used to be the beauties of their years. We reached the next street and could hear the wailing and howling.

Oh my god! Lila grandma has already passed away, how terrible. I quickened my pace and walked into a house, full of women wailing, crying, and howling. Some of the Indian funerals can be loud and noisy. I used to wonder, if the soul does ever leave in peace, with all this wailing and screaming! The men were seated out and nodded to us; we nodded back.

"Come you should also give her a bit of last milk," her son said to grandma.

68 *Spices Are Sweet*

If there is an extremely elderly person on their deathbed, milk is given to the person as a last cup of tradition. This custom is sometimes misused in some places, where the milk is given to the dying person at a rate, which cannot be handled. They are force fed and choked to death, I remember witnessing this when I was about nine years old at a distant relative's house. I knew it was wrong, but there were quirks within some people.

We walked into the room, where Lila was lying still, with drops of milk all over her mouth. There were far too many women inside. I broke into a sweat inside the room. The windows were closed and the fan was off. The women howled louder, when we went in and thrust a glass of milk in her direction.

"If we give her another drop of milk, she will choke to death, please open the windows and switch on the fan," grandma instructed.

There was pin drop silence, if they were wailing in agony over losing their loved ones, just a second ago; they are able to respond with silence I thought.

"You don't have to tell us what to do," said Lila's daughter-in-law a portly woman.

Oh great, again in the middle of some drama with grandma. Papa is going to be pissed, I thought fleetingly.

"You know nowadays it becomes a police case, if you suffocate old women and choke them with milk. They will arrest the daughter in laws first," grandma said in a firm voice.

"She can't look for a proposal for her granddaughter, she comes to poke her nose into other people's business," muttered some woman from behind.

I put my head down in shame with nothing else left to do. I mean I could not seriously get up and shout about my rotten luck in the men's department now, could I?

"Yes we know how you choked your mother in law to death," spat out grandma.

Oh boy, we were in the middle of a real battle now. Lila's son walked in.

DD 69

"You should mind your own business," he said, and I saw a few more men walk in.

"You see Lila changed her last will last week. We did not go to the temple, but we went to see a city solicitor," grandma dropped the bomb.

There was a shocked inhalation of many breaths. Her son stared at grandma, and a whisper broke out in the crowd.

"I knew it, I knew your mother was going to put us out on the roads," the daughter in law started raving.

"I want the gold bangle with red stones," said a woman (must be her daughter).

"You won't even get a stone, if you all don't behave yourselves and give us some peace now," said grandma. "All of you now go back home, there is no funeral in this house."

Everyone looked at each other and did the head-nodding thing. Grandma did a shooing motion. The crowd left, Lila's son just stood there not knowing what to do. Grandma showed her eyes to the fan, and he immediately rushed to switch it on.

"Look grandma, Lila grandma is trying to say something," I said.

Lila was with her hand flailing a little beckoning us over, with a smile. We went close to her; she showed the chair in front of her to grandma and signalled me to sit next to her in the bed.

"Don't speak anything!" Grandma told her and smiled holding her hands. Grandma gently wiped the milk trickling down Lila's Face.

I saw a teardrop roll down the wrinkled face of Lila and my grandma held her hands tightly. I cried in silence. I was happy to have such a strong woman like my grandma with me and felt terribly sad at Lila's dilemma.

Seated inside that room, watching the two older women, I wondered if I would also be like this, another fifty years down the line. I shuddered and shook myself; I had a long way to go. I will never grow old like this, I thought with a smile. I would be out of this place, in the city and definitely on a cruise with my best friends.

Chapter 13 - KumKum / Vermillion

Grandma was in a pensive spirit on our way back. I think she was terribly upset with Lila grandma's dilemma. I was worried about what would happen when my parents found out the little scene that happened back there. Now how many things my young brains have to worry on a daily basis? We have the spectacle of people trying to stifle an old woman, my only sister wanting to kill me and my inability to attract a decent proposal.

My mom was waiting outside the gate; she reminded me of the guards who stand by in protection. She pounced on us as we approached.

"Why did you go there to do unnecessary mitigation? Lila's daughter in law called and complained about you. They also asked why we are sending Santhoshi with you as an assistant. My poor daughter has to go out with you and enter into such grief about being cursed," said mom directly with a pained look.

Grandma just ignored her and walked into the house. I followed her in, with nothing else left to do.

"You have gone to the lawyer. We trust you in old age to go to the temple, but you have gone to change the will. Your son is going to be disappointed with you for going to a lawyer, taking our daughter to Lila's house and me for not controlling you," mom continued.

"Control? You want to check your mind from listening to your older daughter's madness and other people's talk," grandma said in a terribly stern voice.

"Who listens to me, I am only trying to help," mutters mom eager to get in the last word.

"Let's eat lunch," says grandma.

Even if there is some sort of domestic problems, we always make sure that we eat our lunch on time. I loaded my plate with rice, *rasam* and potato curry. I watched grandma help herself with the same. I could hear my mom on the phone and her excited voice. Mom must be talking to her relatives, she sounded happy.

"She is talking to her relatives," grandma mumbled.

We finished our lunch and washed our fingers. I was wondering what to do with the rest of the day. All this free time and nothing to do was a bit boring.

"Your aunt was on the phone, she said we must subscribe to '*the book*' and give your details," mom gushed.

I looked at mom in confusion; mom had a gleam in her eyes.

"Good idea, why did we not think of it, we must advertise about Santhoshi in the community '*book*', grandma said.

Quickly grandma and mom were discussing the enormous merits of '*the book.*' It's funny how women who disagree bond quickly and become allies as quick as the weather. '*The Book,*' this sacred book is not a religious sort, but another brilliant ploy for matrimonial advertisements. You could wonder what is the difference between looking at a newspaper matrimonial, or an Internet matrimonial site. Well, the *book* is printed by some older people in the community and exclusive only to the community members. So you can find about your community members easily. Well, you can call it a sort of community compendium!

Mom and grandma were off on a tangent about how many marriages came about from the *book* and how they know who prints it. They were huddled at the phone again, calling them about enrolling me and putting my wonders down.

"What is your height?" mom shouts from the phone.

"Uhm I am not quite sure," I mutter

"What about the weight?" she asks and drops a tone and whispers, "describe five kilos less."

72 *Spices Are Sweet*

Geez mom I feel flattered.

"Very fair like milk," mom says into the phone.

"Don't lie Latha, state average colour like sand," my grandma says.

"Very beautiful" continues mom.

"Beautiful," says grandma.

I just stand there staring at them. Then we were back in the search with a bang.

"We are getting this month's edition from your aunt now. We can go through it and call up a few people and check their interest," said mom.

"I brought the *book*," my aunt screamed walking in, followed by three of my cousins Shravan, Sarita and Krish (who hides in bushes).

That took them less than a minute to get off the phone and rush here. My family is filled with women who multitask, my aunt managed to speak on the phone, signal one cousin to get a three-wheeler. Lock up her house and load three kids and herself to get here.

"You came so quickly Radha," my mom said excitedly.

"We took *the book* and caught an auto (a three wheel taxi) to come here soon," Radha replied with a big smile.

"We can provide Santhoshi's details on the internet also," said my cousin Shravan.

Shravan is a *Tech Geek*, who just finished his computer degree. The geek look and degree have no relevance; he was always geeky.

"Internet," mom and grandma shouted.

"No we don't want Santhoshi's photo to be sent all over the world. They might take off her clothes and make her look some immoral woman and send it to some other people," mom continued in a disgusted tone.

My aunt quickly closes Krish's ears. There was a silence and my cousins started staring at me first and burst out giggling. I mean seriously, as if my ego has not taken enough bashing for the day. Mom has to offer the idea of morphing my photo and sending it around

"Very sad if we have to look at a computer to look for a groom for Santhoshi," my aunt continued shaking her head in slow motion.

"No, they have your book on the computer. We can still look for a groom all same, same. Santhoshi help me here," my cousin Shravan said looking at me with a smile.

"I have not exactly ever visited a matrimonial site. Let's go there too," I said.

"I found him," screamed mom, peering into *the book*.

"Let me look," my aunt joining in.

Grandma also looked into *'the book'* with an interest, but I am sure she could not see anything without her glasses on.

"Not one, we found so many," my aunt screamed.

Right from being man-less, I have acquired a dozen, just in a moment of peering into a book.

"We will call them now," mom says.

"Don't you think you should talk to Papa?" I ask her.

"Your poor mother, she does so much for you and all the time ask Papa is all you have to say?" Mom was doing her acting bit here.

"Load your laptop let us check out who's in there," continued Shravan.

So that is how my evening ended, with the elders looking at *'the book'*, getting overly excited, my cousins and I huddled up in front of the computer.

We begin our search with a site *"hindugroom.com"*. I must say there were at least 150,000 eligible bachelors in there. There were so many success stories. Seriously, my parents have been wasting their time getting the other guys to come home. This is the *Gita*, (Hindu sacred book) of marriage fixing.

74 *Spices Are Sweet*

There were a variety of 200 single, community men from all over the world. So we proceeded to open the ones with photos. I must say we were silenced again. I may be no prize catch, but this was dreadful stuff. Three guys looked like goons in a sleazy Indian movie. Two guys looked as if they had finished writing a Nobel Prize thesis. The others just looked like the relatives we don't talk to anymore (yes we have quite a few who have no connection with us).

"Can we put up your profile?" asked Shravan.

"Dude, I don' think I feel comfortable with putting up my photo and luring a man through a matrimonial site," I said.

"Let's just create an account and not put your photo," he said.

"We are calling them," screams mom with '*the Book*' in one hand and phone in the other.

My aunt and cousins all huddled around her; I was alone again with the laptop staring at this little spectacle.

"Hello Hello I am Mrs. Latha, I am calling about your boy P," mom said.

Shravan quickly put the speaker on so that we could hear the rest of the conversation.

My aunt looked so pleased that her son was doing such technologically advanced things, like listening to conversations from a telephone speaker.

"Yes yes P, tell me madam," a male voice booms.

"We are calling about our daughter Santhoshi, we are looking for a good alliance and we saw 'the book,'mom continues.

"Yes yes madam," he continues.

"My daughter, she did a degree and finished it. We are remarkably respectable family, and we have connections with the temples and ministers also," mom jabbers on.

"Yes, excellent, excellent," he says.

"Ask them to send the horoscope," interrupts grandma.

Good job grandma, I mean seriously mom had to be stopped.

"Horoscope madam?" he asks.

"Yes P's horoscope," mom says.

"Who madam, who is P?" he retorts.

We all look at each other.

"We are calling from *the book* P is 27 years old, and has a job in Bangalore," mom continues.

"Good, good," he says.

"So are you P's father? mom asks.

"Who is P?" he replies.

My cousin grabs the book and reads out the phone number and asks is this the number.

"Sorry wrong number," says the guy.

Mom now hangs up the phone and says, "I knew it was some wrong dialling." We had to break up for a cup of coffee; everyone was tired after all this talking and excitement. I signalled my cousins that enough of the laptop for the day. I mean I don't want to stare at strange men's photos for the rest of the day.

We were having coffee and discussing the next outing to the movies in the village. The maid came running in to say we have visitors.

"Santhoshi go and see who it is," said mom who was busy eating *pakodas* (batter-fried onions) with her sister and grandma.

I walked into the living room and came face-to-face with Vidya's parents and three of their relatives, dressed in their best clothes with an enormous plate filled with *betel* leaves, betel nuts, *kum kum* and sandalwood paste. They had come to give the wedding invitation.

I did the hand clasping *namaskaram* and asked them to sit.

"Santhoshi, are you still talking to the milkman," asked Radha aunt, with a fit of giggles from my cousins.

Vidya's parents looked at me in puzzlement. I just smiled like an idiot and rushed in to shut my family up before they caused more trouble.

"Vidya's parents are here to give wedding invitation," I told mom.

Mom stopped eating and did an eye thing to her sister and grandma. Mom must have grown up watching some old detective movie, because she had practiced the art of waggling her eyebrows very well. They quickly got up, wiped their hands on their clothes, and rushed into the living room. Mom signalled me and my cousins to stay in, and not come out.

Chapter 14 - Onion

We could hear the brief conversation between the adults in hushed whispers. Mom and the crowd were putting up a display of having high elite silent conversations. When they wanted to, the women could speak in hushed tones.

"Santhoshi get some coffee," screamed mom.

"No, no, we are leaving don't worry" I heard a woman's voice loud to match moms screaming.

So the invite party left quickly. Mom, grandma and aunt came rushing in, with a card each in their hands.

"Santhoshi, how do you know this boy?" mom asks suspiciously.

"Which boy ma?" I ask in astonishment.

"The bride groom, his people have told Vidya's parents to tell us that the invite is from them also. The groom knows you extremely well," mom looked pained.

"This groom was not even in Santhoshi's college he was in another university," said aunt Radha peering at the card.

In the wedding invite, it is necessary; to put down what degrees you have and maybe throw in the college name for further information. As if people are going to be bothered to read where you studied. Then again, most Indians are inquisitive and like to know where you did your schooling and which university you attended.

I was thinking hard how to answer this. All faces were peering at me pointedly waiting for an explanation. We were all looking at each other.

78 *Spices Are Sweet*

"What is happening here?" Papa said walking in with Anish.

Mom immediately proceeded to give a recap with the outline of my secret alliance with the groom. Seriously, mom made it seem suspicious. Now, my dad and brother were looking at me. With all this time to lapse, truly the little mind should have come up with some sort of explanation.

"He must have been in the office that you did the project in your final year of undergraduate," Anish said.

Uhm what was he, now all of us turned to look at him. He was in turn looking at me. All this was interrupted with the arrival of my sister and her family. All attention shifted there, and everyone surrounded her. Quick visit by Nandini consecutively spelt trouble, her looking pleased with herself could only cause more trouble, and the whole family here as well could cause a catastrophe.

"I was helping you out sis," whispered Anish.

Oh so that's what he was talking about the project and information. I looked at him thankfully and did the thumbs up sign.

"Raj's marriage just got fixed, we went to see a bride, and it was immediately fixed. Wedding in the next two weeks," Nandini said, with a big smile to my mom.

"That's good news; we just got Vidya's wedding invite also. So many weddings," mom said excitedly.

"No wedding in your house ma," Nandini made her point.

The men's folk moved to the living room, and women all surrounded Nandini to find out what was the deal. How much jewellery was the bride going to bring, where was the wedding, how did they find her, how is the family. I just stood there in silence and did not produce any inputs to the proceeding. Of course, no one asked me for any, so I stayed still watching.

After half an hour of discussion, coffee and eating all the left over onion *pakodas*. My parents were trying to convince them to stay for dinner. I watched my sister make such a fuss about how much of work she has before the engagement, which was in three days. It would make someone wonder that she was going to get up and make the bloody ring. She made it sound like a big deal. Mom was busy listening to her talk and trying extra hard to please her.

"*The Book*, you are trying to look in that to find someone for madam," Nandini said with a smirk voice.

The woman had eyes of an eagle I must say. Then again, it was there, right in the middle of table for the whole world to see.

"Yes we don't know what to do," replies mom sadly.

"Yes we have to get her fixed know," continued aunt.

"Santhoshi has this luck with her. Whoever comes to see her gets fixed quickly. She is the lucky charm for all men who want to get married. Always the girl to see, but not the girl to be wedded," Nandini said looking at me pityingly.

"Shut up Nandini. That's enough," said grandma.

I got up and walked upstairs to the rooftop.

"I was telling the truth that you are all not seeing. This morning she said no and in the same evening we fixed Raj," Nandini said loudly.

I was terribly upset although I knew I should not be. I walked into the rooftop and watched the sun set slowly. The maid was taking away the dried clothes, which were hanging on the rope. She proceeded to collect the *vathal* (dried up papads) which had been left to dry on the floor. I sat on the ledge of the rooftop, smelling in the fragrance of the jasmine flowers.

Could what my sister had pointed out to be true, am I having some unlucky spell or something. The plot of the story was I would be hitched soon as the first guy walks in for the bride viewing. I had prayed that I should get married and live happily. I felt genuinely sad and upset. Maybe I should have just married Raj I thought. I shuddered at the theory and realised I am better off alone.

I got off the ledge and started practicing yoga. I found it difficult to do many repetitions of the *Surya namaskar*. With so many days of eating and doing nothing, I was getting unfit and fat.

80 *Spices Are Sweet*

I realised I had to do something to kill time. This idling time had to be stopped. I would do a correspondence MBA. I felt so happy when this idea came in the midst of my yoga session.

"Are you ok," Anish had come up and was watching me.

"Yeah I am good, bit unfit," I said getting up from the floor.

"I heard what Nandini said; you should not let her get to you."

"I don't care what she says, it doesn't matter really. I think I will do MBA by correspondence," I said.

"Wow, that's great. It will be good for you to be busy. How do you know Karthik?"

"Karthik is a dear friend."

"You had an affair with him?" my brother asked.

I burst out laughing and continued until I had tears in my eyes.

"You know what my little brother it would have saved me a lot of trouble if I had," I said.

My brother just shook his head slowly in confusion. It was dark, and fireflies were lighting up the rooftop like little stars.

"*Amma* is calling you," the maid came up to get us.

After dinner, I went to Papa to ask about my studies.

"Yes that will be good; you should do your MBA by correspondence. We don't want you to go away to the university right now. We are looking for your partner, and if we find the right guy, then it will interrupt your studies," he said.

"What another degree? Already with one degree, it's difficult to find someone. If she has two degrees, then the boys with one degree will say no to her," mom interrupted from her eavesdropping station.

"Let her start this by correspondence, and we will see what happens," papa said finally.

I rushed outside and quickly texted to Maya. I was doing something finally. Grandma seemed pleased, so was Anish.

My mobile rang. It was Maya.

DD 81

"Great I am happy you are doing something. How are you?" she asked.

I told her about the happenings of the last days, and she was listening intently.

"I will be coming to your place to go for Karthik's wedding, my parents don't seem too keen, and they don't even know them that much."

"Yes, come here I am so bored. The only company I have around here are my cousins, grandma, my family, aunts, uncles, cows and goats. Not necessarily in that order," I said.

"You have so many people around you," she said laughing.

We said bye after a little more of chatting. I noticed a text message unread on my mobile after hanging up.

It was Karthik "How are you? Did you get the card?"

I called him up. I don't know why I did that but just dialled his number. He seemed surprised to hear from me.

"Hey, how are you? I did not expect a call."

"I am good. Why shouldn't I call you, now that you are getting hitched?"

"Hey you can call me anytime. I wanted my parents to send you a card, but Vidya said her parents are inviting you too."

"Yes thanks for nothing; I had a lot of explaining to do about how I know you. I had to make up something."

"Oh, sorry. I think I did not think!" Karthik was blabbering.

"Yes I know you can't think. I am going to do my MBA by correspondence."

"Wow, congratulations, you sure can kill time, until you meet your match."

I was speechless. Is that what I was trying to do? Kill time until I find the man of my life. I was totally confused, with my life. My silence was an inspiration for him to talk about how marvellous it was going to be at the wedding. I interrupted and said I had to go as mom was calling.

Chapter 15 - Salt

Few Weeks later.

I had enrolled for my MBA and started the coursework. My days were frantic with studying and learning to cook. I might be more of a saleable person if I could actually cook and not let mom lie about my skills in the kitchen. The first few days were disastrous while making a *dosai* (a rice flour pancake). My *dosai* were in every conceivable shape, except the shape they ought to be – round like a full moon! And to add to that my curries were unique – either too spicy, or too salty – never the right proportion to eat. What was even worse, they did not even look good I had burnt a few dishes in the kitchen. The *chapattis* (wheat tortillas) were hard and brittle. Still I had faith that it would improve in time.

My mind was also occupied with studying. I realised it had been slowly but surely rusting away when I was doing nothing. We were leaving for Chennai tomorrow, and Maya was arriving tonight. I was happily excited at the idea of going for the wedding for three whole days, and I could get some shopping done. With this thought, I looked at the shoe cupboard; my espadrilles sandals were lying so lost and forlorn. They had not seen daylight for a long time. It was of course impossible to wear them and run around in the village.

The man search had been active; we received inquiries from the online matrimonial site. I must be one hot chick, since fifteen men responded to my profile and only one has been chosen from the pool to be met up with. Strangely, the Scientist S had put in a request that he would see me in Chennai at a coffee shop; I like the guy already. My parents who are extremely conservative and backward in this aspect, surprisingly agreed to this little meeting. I would like to say that my parents were becoming *"new age,"* stealing words from my mom, but I think it might have to do with a couple of the relatives suggesting that I was not getting any younger.

My parents looked terribly worried and tired these days. They were changing their mindset and trying to adapt to the modern times, to this new age. If someone had suggested a meeting at a coffee shop a few years back, I am sure they would have just said no. Now that they are opening, their mind to saying yes to this meeting was a sure sign that things were perhaps, in an advantageous situation for me.

The latest match was a Scientist. Let's call him S from France. We would go for Karthik's wedding in Chennai and a coffee meet up with S, would be arranged later during the day. Maya would accompany me and sit through the coffee, so that there is no scandal. Such as me pouncing on S and such, you know...

Scientist S lived in Paris (right next to the Eiffel Tower according to my aunt), I could see myself going to the Cannes in my little black dress and beautiful shoes. Maybe I should do an Indian touch and go in a Sari. S could come as the crazy scientist to receive the award. Right, he won't be getting any award at the Cannes, but anyway he should be sent an Invite if he was as bright as my relatives keep telling me. Did I mention that my brain was back in action, or should I say functioning again? Oh well.

I heard the toot of a horn and ran downstairs to the entrance to welcome Maya. Mani, Maya's chauffeur kind of smiled at me. There was an indication of a tiny smile, but I might have been very well imagining it. He must have missed me. Maya and I hugged each other tight. She walked in to get accosted by mom, who wanted to know if Maya's parents were in the look out to which laughingly she said not yet. Before I could even attempt to start and tell her about the S and the Eiffel tower, mom had done the needful.

"So you will look at the Eiffel Tower every day eh?" Maya asked me with a sly smile.

84 *Spices Are Sweet*

"Yes we can all look at Eiffel Tower, when we go to visit Santhoshi, maybe you should make a pledge and pray to the tower when you wake up in the morning," mom suggests.

"Mom, why would I pray to the tower when I wake up," I asked her.

"Just a promise you can make to the tower so that you will actually get married and see it every day," mom says.

I could see Maya trying hard not to laugh and biting her lips. She was looking away. I could just imagine myself waking up in the morning and pointing incense sticks in the direction of the tower and possibly ring the bell a bit and chant my morning prayers, all while looking at the Eiffel Tower.

Mom had rushed in to get dinner; Maya was holding her stomach and laughing so hard that tears were streaming down her eyes.

"You will be the first to pray to the tower without fail and recite mantras to it," she said giggling again.

"Shut up," I said in anger stomping upstairs.

Later, that evening we were at the dinner table eating *dosais*. Anish and dad were meeting us in Chennai as they had already left to enrol Anish in College.

"Maya my only prayers these days are to get Santoshi married happily, your poor aunt how many temples I have gone to and prayed," mom starts again.

"Oh aunt don't worry I am sure marvellous things come with time," Maya saintly retorts.

"I am doubtful this will work out," said grandma.

"WHAT." Screamed mom in shock.

"It's Just this feeling I get," said grandma eating her *dosai*.

Mom burst out crying, "You only care about your other granddaughters and not the one who lives with you."

"Oh mom stop that," I say.

"Look at her only supporting you all the time, she does not care about her poor mother," mom continues.

Maya kicks me under the table; she is clearly enjoying this bit of family drama.

"Maybe aunt, she can go up the Eiffel tower and do a *surya namaskar* (Sun salutation) every full-moon day," suggests Maya.

Mom turns off the tap, sorry stops her tears and nods in delight. Grandma also looks on pensively. I just Kick Maya hard but scream "OUCH", since I have somehow managed to kick the chair instead.

Grandma was unusually quiet these days. I think she was missing me already. I kept asking her what it is, but she would only smile and nod her head and do her prayers and stuff. She even stopped telling me stories from the 1950s, which means grandma was not her usually cheery self. I wondered if I should tell her that France was not too far, she could come to visit me. . Somehow, I did not get around to having that conversation.

Maya and mom went through my suitcase to check my clothes; I had packed for the wedding. Not that I needed any help in that department but when you have an overbearing mom and a friend, you have them checking out your clothes and accessories all the time. For meeting up with S, I told mom that I could not bear to go in a Sari to the coffee shop.

"I will wear a lovely *shalwar* mom, I am going to a coffee shop," I said.

"What will they think of you? Going for the bridal viewing in pants," mom said.

"I am not going in pants, these are Indian clothes too."

"Aunt let her wear a *shalwar kameez*," Maya butts in.

"Ok honey, if you say so," says mom.

Maya gives me a smug smile, and I just shook my head.

Chapter 16 - Turmeric

We took the night train to arrive in Chennai early next morning. We were tired and dirty. The busy station was full of activity. It was as if half of Chennai was at the station, pushing, and rushing about their work. My brother was at the station to pick us up. Mom, Maya, grandma and I got off with our suitcases. Mine was the biggest out of the lot and made Anish raise his eyebrow.

"Are you ok grandma?" Anish questioned looking at grandma..

"Ok," grandma replied in one word.

"Did you quarrel with grandma?" Anish whispered to my mom.

"Always blame your poor mother," mom retorted in a voice loud enough to echo through the entire Chennai station. Thankfully, she was interrupted with her mobile ringing and whipped it out to have a hushed conversation in it. Guess it was my sister. Maya and my brother did a head nodding of hellos. My parents owned an apartment very close to Chennai station. We quickly got into the jeep and were on our way. Although, we lived close by, it took us a solid half an hour to get there because Chennai had major traffic jams during peak times.

We had to attend the pre-reception in the evening and wedding early in the morning tomorrow. In our village, we usually have the reception after the wedding. In Chennai and other large cities, it is very difficult to book wedding halls and usually people could book a hall only for a night. Slowly, people were changing their rituals and having a reception the day before the wedding.

Mom told us to rest during the day and be refreshed for the

function in the evening. I did not want to waste the day resting. After a quick shower and a double dose of Coffee, I was ready to explore Chennai. Maya wanted to spend the day in a Spa; I wanted to spend the day in the shops. After ten minutes of arguing, we came to an understanding of half a day shopping and half a day beautifying ourselves.

"Come back at five," shouted mom, as we left.

"I feel like Cinderella's friend," giggled Maya.

We spent another five minutes arguing about which mall to visit. There were far too many choices in Chennai, we finally settled to go to the City Centre shopping Mall. Walking into the mall, the sales signs at most shops caught my attention. We first went into the clothes store. I ran around picking up ten outfits at the same time and rushing into the trial room. The salesgirl stopped me and allowed me only five to try out initially. I must say that sometimes an outfit on display looks better on the rack than when worn by you. After trying on about fifteen outfits and modelling them before Maya, who was trying on a fewer number of clothes, I settled for just three outfits.

At the accessory section, I reached out for a pair of earrings and a clutch bag and saw a girl follow suit. I looked at her, and she smiled at me uncertainly. In her hand, she held the earlier selected 3choices of mine. As flattering, as it was, I was a bit pissed. How could I ask her not to choose the same things that I had selected? I hate people wearing the same clothes and accessories and I am in perpetual fear of running into a room, where someone is wearing the identical clothes and accessories as you. I dropped everything that I had spent the last two hours picking and signalled to Maya that I was ready to leave. Maya was finding the whole scene hilarious.

"You have a stalker girl, who wants to dress like you," she burst out giggling.

"Maybe I have a fashion sense, and I should feel flattered someone wants to copy me."

Maya burst out laughing again, and that is how we ended at our lunch table.

88 *Spices Are Sweet*

"You know, I honestly did not want to come for the wedding Santhoshi, but spending time with you was the reason I came," Maya said.

"Why did you not want to come for the wedding?"

"Karthik hardly bothered to keep in touch or anything. Priya too moved to the states and cannot be bothered to reply any of the emails. When I call she sounds distracted and bored."

"Oh," I Said.

I looked sadly at my Chinese platter lunch and I lost my appetite. It was true; I mean these people change so fast as soon as the word marriage enters their lives. Would I be the same?

" Will you be the same?" asked Maya.

Wait a minute; I was thinking along the same lines. Whose line was it supposed to be anyways?

"No, I won't change I will continue to be the same. I will make time for my friends, except I seem to be missing two of them already," I said.

"Hello Beautiful," I heard a boom of a voice and turned around to face Vikram.

You remember Vikram the *gay prospect* that did not work out, the second man in for the bride viewing. Yes, you probably don't remember, what with all the men running up to our door every week. Now that it did seem a bit sleazy, but you may catch my drift.

I stood up to say, 'hi' properly to Vikram and was stopped by a huge hug from him. Behind him was a grumpy, broody male model.

"This is Maya," I introduced Vik.

"This is John," he retorted pointing at the model.

I reached out my hand, but John just acknowledged with a dismissive nod..

"So what are we doing in Chennai, painting the town red eh?" Vikram continued pulling a chair to sit down.

"We are here for a wedding Vikram," I replied.

"How is the fashion world doing?" Maya asked.

"I am doing OK, things are turning up good, and well you know what, I have invitations for a fashion show to-night why don't you two drop by," Vik said.

"We would love to," jumped Maya.

"The reception is in the evening and my parents won't let us go," I interjected.

"I am sure you can find a way and join the party," smiled Vikram.

John was just standing by the side, looking moody. He did not sit or look interested in us.

"I will see you girls there, come late and you can get into the party," Vik walked off waving bye.

"John's weird isn't he, I am so upset for Vik," I said after he left.

"He has an attitude with an A, Vikram's cute though. I am sure they are happy with each other don't waste your time feeling sorry for them," Maya replied.

"We have to spend more time beautifying ourselves to find a man, if all the handsome men are taken by men," I said.

Maya looked confused for a moment and burst out laughing. We walked into the salon for some serious relaxing and beautifying. We had a manicure, pedicure, blow-dried our hair and even had our makeup done. The result was professional. I felt and looked decent.

Mom had started calling me from three pm saying, "don't be late don't be late," like a chant. We walked into the house, where everyone was ready and mom did a double take.

"Santhoshi you look so pretty, maybe we should get a salon to do your make up tomorrow, when you go to see S," she said.

I smiled and ran into change; I was too much in a good mood to get mad at her. I wore a stunning peacock blue sari with motifs of designs in the border. Maya wore a red and silver sari.

90 *Spices Are Sweet*

"Santhoshi," my dad said staring at me.

"How are you Dad?" I asked.

"Hello uncle," said Maya coming up behind me.

Dad was staring at me for a moment and then quickly recovered his composure to say hello to Maya and talk to her.

"Uncle I have to go say bye to my aunt, who is leaving on the eleven p.m. flight from Chennai airport," Maya said.

"Which aunt?" me, my mom and dad asked at the same time.

"Aunt Viki who is off to the states," she said with a look of innocence.

"Yes you can go my dear take Santhoshi and Anish," my dad replied.

"No uncle let Anish stay at home; we can go with the driver," said Maya.

"No Maya, Anish can drive you both!" said dad with finality.

Anish looked annoyed, but did not say anything. Maya smiled at the success of our little plan. I was a bit worried about my brother when he finds our Aunt Viki diverted to the fashion show. Mom was giving updates on her mobile, about us leaving for the wedding to my sister before we get into the car.

We reached the wedding hall, just in time to coincide with the arrival of the bride and groom. A whole load of relatives were around them, my parents had met someone they knew and were doing the head-nodding thing. Maya and I were peering intently to catch a glimpse of Karthik and Vidya.

There was a boom of a male voice, "Come join in the welcome and smile for a photo!"

The whole retinue turned around and stared at both of us. Uhm Maya and I looked at each other. Karthik did a slight head nod, which was not certainly welcome, or go away. Vidya and the rest of the relatives stared at us. Talk about stealing the show. I quickly shook my head to indicate no it's OK.

"No, come we want to have beautiful girls in the photograph," said another aunt.

I looked at mom and gave her a pained expression. Mom swooped into save us and said, "No no they will go inside," and literally dragged us inside.

Vidya the bride, well she was another piece of work altogether. She was shooting daggers at me. She was wearing an outrageous magenta concoction of a sari, which clashed, horribly with her yellow border and had golden polka dots strewn all over. Her neck was adorned with half a ton of jewellery. The biggest necklace adorned in three different lengths, I felt a crick in my neck looking at that. The damage those gigantic earrings must be causing to her ears is beyond repair. I think the bangles were crass in design. Her eyes were like giant balls, which were, going to pop out.

"She is horrendous looking," whispered Maya urgently.

"Uhm well she could do with some help with the dressing I guess," I said noncommittally.

"And are you blind?" Maya said looking at me. "I am really growing to dislike Karthik; he is such a spineless man. He reacted with us as if we were his parent's guests."

We were interrupted when groups of relatives came to speak with mom and did the head nodding at me and started questioning mom about me.

"How old is she? Are you looking for a groom? Who is the girl with her?"

The best line yet, "Her friend is not our community know?"

Maya whispers, "Are all your community like this?"

"I am sure even your community must be like this," I said smiling smugly.

The bride and the groom *aka* ogle eyes and cowardly man were getting on stage. Karthik looked terrific in his blue kurta, pyjamas. Well whoever did the shopping for Vidya had obviously taken a backstage in Karthik's wardrobe. Under the harsh lights, we could clearly make out that Vidya had rubbed half a kilo of powder on her hands to make it look fairer. There were streaks running on her hands. Her face was over made up and looked

92 *Spices Are Sweet*

artificial. As if she sensed, she looked straight at me with hatred. "Santhoshi did you make a face at her," mom asks me slowly.

"What?"

"She is staring at you."

"I know she is staring at me, but really mom do you think that I am childish to make faces at her?"

"You did make her cry a lot when you were kids."

Maya had clearly cheered up with this little chat and she was giggling.

"Come lets go get something to eat," Maya said.

We got up and strolled towards a small stall serving Tiffin. Tiffin was kesari (sweet with a dose of orange colouring, sugar and ghee) and hot *vadai*. They were serving out coffee, as well.

I turned my back and watched the screen, which had been set up to get a clear view of what the bridezilla was up to. She was still staring at my back. Karthik was looking straight and smiling totally oblivious to his wife's trauma. I saw a woman walk up to the bride and whisper into her ears. She quickly got a hold of herself and turned away from my view and was smiling. The photographer was clicking photos.

The bride and the groom are seated on an elevated stage. The stage has two sets of steps. One for getting on to the stage and the other one, naturally, for coming down. I have seen many stages, but there is nothing like the stage at an Indian wedding. I mean most of the stages have only one set of steps. Guests form a queue, to greet the couple and the first one to be greeted - the groom or the bride depends on whose side they belong to – the groom's side or the bride's side. The guests, irrespective of the fact, of which side they belong to always follow the queue. Well almost always. The close relations and the VIPs are allowed to jump the queue.

The way the stage is managed at the Indian weddings is also unique. No one is allowed to forget the fact that the stage belongs to two different sides – the bride's side and the groom's side. And they are always there to defend their territories.

Invariably , two relatives, from each side of the groom and bride, stand next to the couple. They are sometimes parents' of the couple , or if they are busy, they are the close relatives of the couple. They are there to introduce the couple to the relatives, friends etc. Being the senior people, they know about the who's who of the relations and generally introduce the guests to the couple. They also serve another important and practical aspect. These relatives, also known as relations , standing on either side of the groom or the bride are the *treasurers of the gifts also known as presents*. The 'treasurer of the gifts' has to ensure that gifts are transferred to specific suitcases – the bride's side or groom's side. After the ceremony, mothers on both side would carefully note down the details of the gifts or more specifically the value or cost of the gift. These, in the future, would serve as guide for 'returning the gift'. Very practical, I must say. You do not want to return the gift more expensive than you have received. If you have received a gift worth Rs 100, you do not want to give a return gift worth more than Rs 100, whenever you are invited to attend a wedding in their family. You see, we Indians are very practical!

Moreover, those who gave the gifts, invariably noted down the worth of the gifts for future reference. So that they could compare the value of the so-called returned gift

The guests were making a beeline on the stage to wish the couple and take a picture with them. The long queue was ever growing. I took a plate of Tiffin to give it to grandma who was sitting with all the older women and having a chat.

Both of us were introduced to all of grandma's friends, half of whom I knew and some I did not. I did the *namaskar*, and Maya nodded her head. The chatter of different voices was shattered by a loud roar of music.

Chapter 17 - Saffron

Have you ever experienced an ear piercing music that can be heard by the whole neighbourhood? No, I am not talking about the music we play to annoy the neighbours but something to similar effect. There was a small stage set up for entertainment, which had a singing troupe. We saw the latest craze hit the Indian TV, singers outstanding winners, lined up with a music troupe to sing the entire top twenty in the Indian charts.

They were over dressed, the makeup was too much, and even though the hall was air-conditioned to beat the heat, the entertainers were sweating. The adults were pretty much enjoying the spectacle, which ranged from the latest hits to teasing songs full of enticing meanings for the couple on their first night.

Maya and I giggled and sat down to watch the entertainers and the stage in turns. Our heads just swayed this way and that.

"Don't you love the music, I have taken the artists' business card for your wedding Santhoshi," mom bustled in with a card in hand. "Let us go have dinner and wish the happy couple."

"Well the music is sorted for your wedding hahahaha," giggled Maya.

I just gave her the look, which is supposed to silence her but, had her giggling away. I must say I caught a sight of myself in one of the glasses, I did look absurd and well I broke down laughing, as well.

Mom was annoyed with us laughing like idiots and shooed us on. We went to the stage, which was almost empty by now, since the audience were more interested in ogling at the musicians.

The photographers were getting Vidya and Karthik to pose for photos. Karthik looked uncomfortable, but Vidya was popping her eyes out in full glory (yes I know I am horrible).

They saw us approaching and Vidya's parents came running to talk to my parents, and pose in the photograph. Photographs are usually taken with the respective parents so that there is a list of whose invitees turned up, and parents can refer up if their guests did come. Wedding videos are mostly taken so that the family members can admire themselves in their flashy clothes and jewellery and keep an account of the relatives who turned up and who did not. I am sure you can lose count of who came and did not when you end up inviting about three thousand people. If someone did disrespect you and not turn up for the wedding, you make sure, you don't go for their wedding when they invite you.

Karthik turned and gave us a forced smile and a slight nod. The guy totally looked constipated, and Vidya, well she was peering intensely at my neck. Do I have a love bite or something from a cockroach (I mean seriously, there was no man in the picture so it must be some bug, which bit me) I wondered. My hands were itching to touch my neck and feel if all was OK.

The yellowish tinge in her face was visible close up, she must have had the turmeric bath to prepare herself for the wedding. There were tiny patches of yellow on her face. Turmeric powder has amazing powers of improving skin colour and removing facial hair. If applied in excess, it could give the look of a patient suffering with jaundice.

"This is Santhoshi, who played with you Vidya!" said her mom.

"This is her best friend Maya," butted in mom.

Then I honestly was frightened. Vidya's eyes were gleaming, with disdain, and contempt. She gave an extremely difficult stiff smile and did a slight head nod, which was there but not there really. I am not making it up, really, she sneered and Karthik and looked all flustered. I turned to look at Maya to make sure that I was not seeing things. I think I share a bond with Maya as she turned and looked at me at the same time (not bond maybe she did feel me turning, but I do like to think I have a bond). The surprise on her face was evident.

"Please, stand straight and smile," screamed the photographer.

We quickly stood beside my mom who unsuccessfully tried to force us next to the bride, and we just moved away to the other side.

"Tell the young girls to stand next to the bride," shouted the photographer.

We were saying no to this and Vidya was scowling even more. Karthik, well! He just pretended not to notice all this happening.

"Just take the photo," shouted Vidya's Mom. "These photographers are always bossing." She screamed louder so that the photographer could hear.

If the photographer heard this bit of insult, he just ignored it. I am sure they deal with bossy wedding parties regularly. We quickly left the stage while mom was busy saying bye bye to the family. Maya and I did not stick to say bye.

"What's on my neck?" I whispered to Maya while going down.

I knew Vidya was staring at me from the stage, I could certainly feel the stare of hot rocks piercing my back.

"That one!" Pointed Maya.

We looked at a still shot in the large TV Screen, in front of us, and there we were. Maya, I smiling, and Vidya staring at my neck, and lo and behold was having a conversation with my necklace. We started giggling, and we were holding each other and giggling. I must make a point here to let you know a bit about the necklace I was wearing. It was an heirloom piece of sapphire, artfully designed in gold. I had it specially made for me.

"She is talking to my necklace Maya!" I said.

Maya was shaking her head in amusement and turned to look at the stage. Vidya was staring at us with hatred because she had seen us laughing at the screen. I did the most useless thing;

DD 97

I stuck my tongue out at her. She looked shocked and turned to show something to Karthik. I pulled Maya and walked away from the screen and towards the last rows. We were doubled up in laughter.

We approached grandma and helped her get up to go for dinner with her old friends. We made our way to the dinner table and sat down to eat. We were served on a large banana leaf. They served us 16 different types of food; I knew this because they had laid out a little placard with all the food listed. Three sweets, two savouries and three main dishes with accompaniments. I was not hungry but maybe greedy, so tried out a little bit of everything.

"If we attend a few more Indian weddings we will be fat. Stop eating everything Santhoshi," said Maya.

"Mhem," I said, continuing with the eating, the saffron scented dessert was just delicious.

After dinner, we sat around and waited for another half an hour for my parents and Anish to turn up.

"We need to hurry up to get to the fashion show!" said Maya. "We should just go like this, no need to change."

"We can't go to a fashion show like this," I whispered back. "We need to change at least into jeans and T Shirt!"

"That not going to happen, you will be bringing unwanted attention to yourself if you change," said Maya.

I just shook my head and looked at the scene where Vidya and Karthik were seated and whispering to each other. I thought of Scientist S who I am supposed to meet tomorrow. Will I be sitting like that soon if he says yes. These days, the marriage act was causing me to think a little. I had all these 'what if questions,' which I had not had all these years. What if I don't like him? What if I am disappointed for the rest of my life? What if he cheats on me? Yes, these questions were frightening.

At last, we managed to leave the wedding hall at ten thirty and reached home around eleven.

"Maybe I will also come to say bye to your aunt," started mom.

98 *Spices Are Sweet*

"No aunt you rest now, the wedding is there tomorrow morning," Maya was quick.

"I don't want to come for the wedding tomorrow," I said.

There was silence, we were all seated in the van and not got off yet.

"Why you come all the way to Chennai for your friend's wedding and you don't want to come?" mom questioned.

"I don't want to come for the wedding too," said grandma.

"Oh yes you join your granddaughter and be up to her ways. Maya has come all the way to participate in the wedding ceremony, so she will know what your wedding is like" continued mom.

"Enough," said dad. "Maya do you want to go to the wedding tomorrow?"

"Uncle it's been very tiring today; I don't want to go for the wedding," said Maya.

"Ok, you can stay at home, we will go with Anish," said dad.

Mom looked annoyed; I know she will be up early to tell Nandini about this turn of events.

"Anish take them to say bye to Mayas aunt and bring them home safely," said dad.

Mom got off without saying bye and grandma just smiled and followed her. Anish took over the wheel from the driver, and Maya jumped to join him in front.

"Anish change of plans, you have to drop us off at the Rapton hotel," said Maya.

"What, you are both going clubbing, are you? I am not taking you," scowled Anish.

"You sure are, you can meet up for coffee with your friends. We are just going for a friend's fashion show and you will pick us up?" said Maya.

"Santhoshi, you have to see the prospective groom tomorrow. If you are running around in the night like this, it will create a scandal." Anish turned around from the wheel and looked at me.

DD 99

"Your sister's last wish before marriage is to attend the fashion show, can't you do this for me?" I pleaded.

Poor Anish was stumped for a moment; I made it sound like a death wish. He gave out a sigh of resignation and turned the van. Maya winked at me.

"So you drop us off at the hotel, meet up with your friends and call us when you are done. Or you could come with us and we will try to take you in," Maya said.

"No I am not coming, hope you don't get into trouble," Anish said.

We were in Rapton Hotel quickly. We get off, and I turn and look at my brother. He smiles slowly, and I know it's OK with him. We walk into the lobby after the checking and move towards the hall where the fashion show was held, only to see people walking out. Maya and I look at each other.

"The fashion show?" Maya starts to one of the guys.

"It was over ages ago," he says.

"The after party?" Maya says.

"Its upstairs in some of the rooms, I doubt you can get in," he says.

"Come let's go," Maya drags me to the lift.

"Fashion show party upstairs," she says to the burly lift guy.

"Not allowed," he says and looks away.

"We have invites," Maya continues.

"No special invites madam, and No!" He says.

We see a girl in an ill-fitting leather mini skirt, spaghetti top and bad boots walk past, and he waves her into the lift.

"You are not letting us in because we are in Indian clothes," Maya splutters in anger.

The bouncer ignores us, and Maya tries to charge into the lift dragging me behind. The guy quickly steps in and drags us out. Oh god, I am so embarrassed.

"I said no madam!" he said.

100 *Spices Are Sweet*

"Call Vik quick," Maya says to me.

I drag her and quickly move to a corner and try his mobile. It rings and rings and rings.

"Let's try the stairways," says Maya moving towards to the stairways where a burly man is standing with a scowl.

"Let's just go home Maya," I say. "Let's call Anish!"

"Oh what a sad evening, let's go have a drink at least," Maya says with a sad face.

So we walk into the coffee shop and sit down, and open the menu.

"Can we have two glasses of the red please?" Maya says.

"Sorry madam, no alcohol after eleven, would you like some juice or coffee?" says the waiter.

Maya turns and looks at me in shock.

"Give us a moment," I say to the waiter.

"Maya, they don't serve any alcohol after eleven in Chennai," I say to her.

Maya puts her head down on the table and stays there for a minute. I start laughing. I mean seriously the night could not get worse.

"I need something strong, this is damn ridiculous. No fashion show, no after party and no alcohol," she says.

"Maya!" a girl comes running to our table and Maya gets up to hug her, they quickly break off into Telugu, and chat for a full five minutes.

I saw the waiter stare at our table, he must be wondering at which point we were going to order.

"Santhoshi we are in luck, meet my friend Jenny," Maya says signalling me to the girl.

I said a hello, had a short introduction to Jenny, Mayas friend from school. She was going to friends for a drink and invited us to join.

"Uhm Jenny I just met you, and to come to your friends, Uhm thanks but it's ok "I said.

"Oh no, Maya's friend is my friend, my friends are your friends,'" Jenny said smiling.

"I am not going home without a drink," said Maya and quickly moved onto the group who were standing there and started introducing us.

Chapter 18 – Betel Nut

I was seated squashed between Maya and some guy we had just met, in a jeep and were on our way to another friend's house. This was outright ridiculous, it was nearly twelve. I was a bit worried when exactly we would be going home, about Anish, who was under the impression that we are in Rapton hotel. These guys were going around in circles in the neighbourhood looking for the address of the friend's house.

"You don't know the address of your friend's house?" I asked the guy.

"It's a friend of a friend, we don't know him!" He said.

Oh boy, oh boy. I looked at Maya, who pretended she had not heard.

We finally managed to locate the friend's house and landed at the apartment. A guy came over to open the gate. About ten of us got off including me, Maya and Jenny. The majority of girls and guys seemed genuinely friendly although we had just met them. I guess I could count this as one of the strange nights in my life.

"Hi I am Sanjay," said the host. "Do not make too much noise and wake up the neighbours SH."

We walked up slowly, Maya and Jenny were giggling, and I just trudged behind them. Half of us were in. Suddenly, Maya and Jenny screamed and ran behind me. I turned to see what it was; it was an enormous animal or something like that. It came straight at me, held me with its paws, and pushed me against the wall.

"This is Misty," said Sanjay. "Hope you guys like dogs."

DD 103

Misty held me tight and started sniffing my private parts. I am a person, who is terrified of dogs and Maya more so.

"Can you take her?" I started, and misty brought her face real close to mine.

I closed my eyes and tried to move her away; Misty became wilder and tried to put her nose up my backside. I screamed in fright.

"She is scared of dogs," Maya said urgently to Sanjay.

"Oh but she is just being friendly. Don't struggle," he said.

I was struggling, and Misty was getting friskier with me. The neighbours' switched their lights on.

"Stop that noise," shouted a sleepy uncle from inside.

"SHHHH," Sanjay said, and he tried to pull Misty away with the help of a friend. Now all of them were looking at me..

After five long minutes of struggle, and the Labrador smelling and licking me all over, they took Misty away.

"Oh are you ok?" Maya and Jenny came up to me.

"NO I am not ok, I want to go home," I said with a stammer.

"Let's go in," they said dragging me in, totally ignoring the fact that I was traumatised.

Misty was trying to jump on everyone there and came up to me wagging. I did not sit, but misty could stand. I hid behind Maya.

"It's rude, this guy loves dogs, and we are scared, we must leave Maya," I whispered to her.

Maya screamed in terror, and was struggling, to drag Jenny in front of her. A shuffle, brawl and screaming by Jenny and Maya, I stayed strong and stubborn near a wall refusing to move forward.

"Sanjay we are calling it a night," said Jenny. "You guys stay on I will drop them home."

Misty had to be forcibly taken, away from us, and she looked sorry that I was leaving. I ran downstairs in relief.

104 *Spices Are Sweet*

"Phew!" I said coming out.

"I am scared of dogs too," said Jenny.

"I am terrified, but Santhoshi seems to attract them all the time. There was this one day, we were going for a lunch, and a bunch of stray dogs came and licked her," said Maya.

WOOF WOOF! I turned to see two strays approaching me, I ran and got into the vehicle with Maya and Jenny following me.

"Can you drop us home please?" I asked Jenny, who nodded.

"What a night?" said Maya looking at me.

We burst out laughing nonstop. Jenny looked at us puzzled. I was laughing so much that I had tears in my eyes. I have no idea why I was laughing, but it had been a crazy night. Jenny dropped us off with hugs and promises to meet up soon. We texted Anish that we were home, and to get back quickly.

The next morning we woke up to find grandma at home. Mom, dad and Anish were at the wedding.

"Why did you not want to go to the wedding grandma?" I asked her.

"I saw Vidya staring at you," said grandma smiling.

"Grandmas exceedingly clever Santhoshi," said Maya.

"Santhoshi you should have less expectation in your life," grandma said to me seriously.

"Oh grandma, I did not expect anything from Vidya," I argued.

"It is not Vidya, I am talking about, in life if you don't have any expectation, things will be easier for you to manage," she said patting my hand.

"I think it's a coded message," Maya whispered as we watched grandma walk away.

"I know it's coded, the thing is I have no idea how to de-code the message," I looked helplessly at Maya.

The rest of the day was spent lounging around and watching TV. My parents arrived back after lunch and looked tired.

DD 105

"Did they ask for us?" I asked my mom.

"No, no they did not ask for you, now we have a problem again. The bride viewing has been switched from the Coffee shop to your dad's long lost relative's house. Now you can't go to the salon," mom continued.

I watched grandma and my dad having a conversation in hushed voices near the kitchen. Maya raised her eyebrows, I raised mine back. I was looking forward to the coffee shop meeting, but I guess we are going somewhere else.

"We have to adjust. Blah blah blah," mom was saying to my dad.

"Enough." My dad silenced her and my grandma, came out, and just looked at me.

"Get ready it takes an hour to get to Vellachery, to your Uncle Narayan's house," said grandma.

"I will get some flowers for your hair," announced grandma walking out of the apartment.

"We are going to a long lost relative's house mom, why can't they come here?" I asked my mom.

"Your poor mother, does anyone discuss these matters with me, No," mom said with a sniff.

"It is your relatives who got the proposal mom," I said.

"Yes, just blame me," and mom huffed off.

"Your mom is such a drama queen," Maya said.

"Get Ready! QUICK," shouted mom.

So we set off to get ready, I wore the Sari, which I wanted to wear to the wedding, and set about doing my makeup.

"So why don't you just wear the *Shalwar Kameez*?" asked Maya.

"I am going to my relatives' house, we don't want a so called scandal starting and to lose S, as I did not wear the right clothes, now do we?" I asked with a smile.

"How do you do it?" Maya asked.

"Do what?"

106 *Spices Are Sweet*

"Keep up your sense of humour with all this, aren't you scared?"

"I am really scared, petrified with what the future holds for me. You know what I am more scared of? Disappointing my parents by not getting picked in the marriage market," I said with a smile.

Maya hugged me tight and wished me luck. We ran downstairs and found my family again in a secret meeting. My dad, grandma and brother were on one side and mom on her mobile.

"Let's go," dad announced with certainty and off we were.

I walked out of the house and was stopped short with a large black cat crossing my path.

"OH MY GOD. What bad luck! We must go in and have a cup of water," she said.

If a black cat crosses your path, it is supposed to be a bad luck. Therefore, to ward off the karma, we had to go back inside the house and drink a glass of water. Dad and grandma looked terribly upset by this.

"It's ok; we can fix this if Santhoshi comes across a cow," mom announced.

Oh, yes, if a cow crosses your path its good luck, as opposed to the cat. Maya looked in amazement at this conversation. She was trying hard not to laugh.

"This is Chennai, where are we going to find the cow?" my dad asked.

"Yes, yes if it were home, we could have asked someone in the village, to bring a cow to the entrance," mom replied sadly.

"I think you should cross Santhoshi's Path before we leave," suggested grandma to mom.

I saw Maya do a double take at this and my whole family jumped up with enthusiasm. I was trying hard not to laugh, because I knew Maya was getting more and more flummoxed by my family.

We moved out again and mom did a bit of walking in front of

me, crossing my path about two times. I was quickly shoved into the vehicle, before any other bad omen should pass.

"Your grandma suggested that your mom walk instead of the cow? What's going on?" whispered Maya.

"Yeah mom did it with great enthusiasm I think," I replied with a smile.

If a married woman crossed your path, it's supposed to bring good luck in bounds, when you are going out. I did not explain this to Maya; I let her think that my mom and the cow shared some bond. We reached the house and were welcomed by many adults. I lost count and could not associate names with faces anymore. I just did the head-nodding thing and Maya kept following my head signs.

The old women in the family were doing their best job of questioning me and mom was busy answering instead of me. Thankfully, we were interrupted, by the arrival of the family. A very pleasant faced uncle and aunt with the groom S and another sweet girl arrived. They all smiled in a friendly manner, and I got up and did the prayer thing. The adults were all introduced; the girl was their elder daughter-in-law. I looked and smiled at her, and she smiled right back. S looked OK; I mean my heart did not go thump thump nor did my stomach do a butterfly flip. He looked straight at me and smiled.

"Can we talk?" he asked to interrupt the adults.

Straight to the point, he was. I looked at my parents, and they nodded. Quickly, we were led to the rooftop of the house. It was beautiful, I could see a little bit of Chennai from this position.

"Do you have any question you would like to ask me?" S said.

I turned and looked at him, as fascinating as Chennai from this rooftop was; I had matters in hand to discuss.

"No, not really," I replied. I had not actually made a list of questions for him; I did not think it was appropriate to ask him about the Eiffel tower at this point.

The next half an hour, S spoke to me pleasantly about his family, his brother, his job. He questioned me about my background

108 *Spices Are Sweet*

and interests. I was explaining about the benefits of yoga, when Maya came to the rooftop and signalled me that mom wanted me downstairs soon. She did this by jumping up and showing the time and signalling downstairs. If Maya stays with us a few days, she will certainly start doing the sign language to the pat.

" Let them know, we will be downstairs in five minutes," said S.

I was willing to be here, all day talking to this S; he was funny and attentive. When I say funny, he did not crack some really rib tickling jokes. He gave me his card and said we can stay in touch through chat.

We came downstairs and he bid goodbye to everyone, and he waved to me. My family gave me a look of disapproval, for the delay on the roof top chat. Mom had become best friends with S's family and was addressing his dad as brother. Grandma and dad were quiet; and watching. Maya was doing the eyebrow thing at me. I hid his card in the palm of my hand, for some reason, I did not tell my parents. Mom would probably take the card and supervise our chat.

We had to wait around another ten minutes, after the S family left and listen to their wonders, from the adults. Maya was more and more bored by the minute. When we said bye the aunt, at the house, gave me a betel leaf with a betel nut, as a return gift, an auspicious mark. As we got into the vehicle, my mom started her hundred questionnaires.

"Why were you so late? What did he say? What did you say?"

I gave her an overview of our chitchat.

"Oh thank you God, I think this is it," mom said happily satisfied with my answer.

When we got home, I gave a recount to Maya and asked her what she thought.

"He seems ok it should work out, and I will be here for your wedding, before you know it. Your mom is hilarious; she was saying glowing things about you and had S's parents eating out of her hand. They have all become the best buddies and relatives," Maya giggled.

I showed her the business card, which was stuck on the palm of my hand.

"Don't mail him first," Maya said.

"Of course not," I said smiling.

"We are going out for dinner to celebrate," said mom bustling into our room.

"Celebrate what mother?" I asked her.

"Celebrate new found relatives and friends," mom replied in delight.

My last night in Chennai, ended with a beautiful dinner with my family and my best friend. There was no mention of the wedding or my proposal, and I was glad of that. Maya was going back home tomorrow, and we had to leave, as well. I honestly looked forward to getting back home and to my routine.

Chapter 19 – Sugar

We were welcomed home with a call from uncle Narayan. S had said he was not interested in the proposal. I think my parents took it better than I did, because I burst out crying, when I heard this. It was not as if I was madly in love with the guy, but it was the fact that I was not going to see the Eiffel Tower soon. Ok, maybe it was also the fact that the geek had refused me, as well. I mean there is nothing wrong with me, except a little bit of craziness.

Uncle Narayan was not happy about S saying no and had reprimanded his parents, and challenged them that I would be married to a better proposal, in the next three months. This information was passed on by my mother to cheer me up. I cried when I heard this. It was as if I was some unsellable product, not moving even during *'sales.'*

Papa said, "Please stop crying, there is something better in store for you."

Grandma said, "You should not waste your tears; I had a bad intuition about it. I also asked you not to have any expectations."

"Grandma, I don't want to hear 'I told you so'," and I wept a bit more.

"From next week, it is inauspicious to look for proposals for a month, so let's take a month's break and try after a month," mom said.

I think mom was flummoxed with my crying, and was handling the situation more calmly. The whole family was handling it

DD 111

with acceptance, and I think the stress of it all was getting to me, and I was depressed. Maybe I was just was suffering from PMS.

I went upstairs and took out my laptop. I know you should never be the first to call a boy, but I did the one thing, which is unthinkable.

I send out a mail to S:

Hi S,

I am not going to ask how you are. I would like you to know that I am shocked that you refused the proposal. What is it that you find in me, which made you refuse me? This is the first time I have failed in my life.

Awaiting your prompt reply.

Ok that was a bit of a lie, about the first refusal, but honestly I could not tell him that I am losing count now of the men turning me down, could I? I felt better after sending the email polishing off a Cadburys Chocolate bar. I needed that.

Maya called me; as usual, mom had updated her.

"I cannot believe you are weeping because someone said no."

"You don't get it Maya; I am tired of all the negative outcomes."

"You are in your twenties, and you are talking as if you are past your sale date."

"Spot on, I feel as though I am past my sale date. I want to get married soon."

"Santhoshi, I feel sorry listening to you. We are in a time where women are taking over the world."

"I don't want to take over the world. I just want to get married."

Ok, did I just say that out, I am actually a confused and desperate soul? Maya hung up after that. There was not much left to say now. I checked my email to see if there was a reply from S. As expected, there was none that day. Or the day after or the day

112 *Spices Are Sweet*

after that. He never did acknowledge my email or reply it. No surprise's there.

The month of mid July to mid-August was inauspicious for any more searches. I was ready to be left alone. The days just passed and I just kept myself busy with the course work. I had an exam to appear for in January. My cooking skill was improving by now; mom was shocked that I was such a talented cook. For me, it was like the Science that I studied in school. You combine the right ingredients, and you get some fantastic results.

Grandma was back to her carefree ways; my parents were getting on with their own work. The little cousins who were always around were busy with school. I spoke to Priya once, she sounded very vague and distracted. When I asked her if she was ok, she replied with false enthusiasm that she was. Maya and I spoke to each other whenever possible. Scientist S was a never discussed subject again. My brother had gone off to University; and was happy there, I think. Since, we hardly heard from him these days.

It was the last day of the religious calendar in the month of August. It usually falls on a no moon day. It was a tradition to pray to the ancestors, who were no more and offer them their favourite food. The house was busy with the preparation for the pooja. My great grandmother, a formidable woman in a photograph, was offered a beautiful green sari. After the prayers, it was sent to young girls in the family, who are awaiting marriage or someone who was pregnant, obviously after marriage. It was a belief that she would bless the girl who gets it.

My sister Nandini had a few of the green versions with her. She always had a need for it to be given to her, since she was burdened, with so many domestic issues. I always thought, she was just eying a free sari. This year *'yours truly,'* was getting the sari as *Good Luck Charm*. We had a tussle for that one, since Nandini wanted it to be given to the new bride of Raj, her brother-in-law.

When this suggestion was brought up, my grandma told Nandini off pretty well. Seriously, this new bride was in no way closely related to us, and she was not a blood relative. Well, that's what grandma said. Mom was as usual, a bit of in confusion; she did not want to disappoint her favourite daughter, but had to agree that perhaps the sari did belong to me. I being single, was in dire need of it.

So it was prayer time in the evening, we were assembled. The beginning was marked, with the ringing of the bell, by my mom. I closed my eyes to concentrate on my prayers, when I heard a shout from the sidelines. An unexpected elderly relative always happens to pop into the prayers. Her name is Pichaiyama, which loosely translated into beggar woman. She is in no means a beggar woman; she is a distant cousin of grandma's. Pichaiyama was there today in a beige sari. I honestly did not know how she was related to us, but she did make occasional visits. She was full of the town and family gossip. She had powdered her face with talcum powder and decorated her forehead with holy ash.

Grandma was mighty pleased with the arrival of her friend and nodded her welcome. Mom looked annoyed with this little diversion, but carried on with her prayer.

Suddenly Pichaiyama let out a shrill cry, closed her eyes, and started speaking rapidly. Grandma held her tight and signalled me to take her other hand. I was petrified and moved to the other end of the room. Mom was excited with this event and papa was guarded. The maids of the house and workers were also staring at this episode with excitement. Pichaiyma had been possessed by the gods or someone else.

"Santhoshi," boomed Pichaiyma.

Oh, bugger! I thought, as luck would have it, it has to be me.

"She is calling you, move forward," nudged mom leaving the prayers midway.

I had to be shoved and pushed forward and Pichaiyma was getting into ecstasy; her eyes looked wild. She was screaming my name and muttering things.

"It is your great grandmother, who is honouring us today with her presence," said grandma in delight.

"Ohhh great mother in law," mom was actually elated.

114 *Spices Are Sweet*

"Yes I am here to say that Santhoshi will marry soon. You have to give me a new sari and a trip to Varanasi," Pichaiyma continued.

"Definitely, we will do that," mom and Grandma said.

"Fall at her feet," whispered mom.

I was struggling now; Pichaiyama had a slight wild look in her eyes. I was a bit scared to do it or not to do it. Therefore, I made a half-hearted attempt of bending, yet, not actually getting there. As I was shuffling toward the floor, Pichaiyma dumped me with a whole load of sacred ash. I stood up straight, and she quickly adorned my face with more. Now mom, grandma were taking turns of getting themselves whitewashed. Papa was beckoned to join the queue and have himself dusted.

I looked at the others they too had a powder coating done. I caught myself in the mirror, I looked worse for wear; a vision showered in white flour. Pichaiyma was slowly coming to her usual sense and performed a fainting act. Mom, grandma and the helpers quickly rushed to her side with water and soothing words.

I tried dusting myself a little here and there, but it was all lost. I would have to be put into an air-drying system to get this out or perhaps, have a bath. I could not actually take off from here yet, since the family was present and we had to finish praying. Mom quickly finished off the prayer. We spent a few minutes more and moved out of the prayer room. Pichaiyma was fanning herself and getting an update from grandma, about her new sari and pilgrimage.

Mom gave a plate first to the visitor, grandma and me, filled with goodies of food offerings from the prayer. Really, we do eat a lot of sweet and fatty food. My great grandma was a woman, who loved her food, which was abundant, in the plate. Sugar *dosa*i (a pancake dusted with sugar and ghee-clarified butter), *seeni urundai* (small ball of sugar, flour and ghee), *payasam* rice pudding, *vadai* (fried dumpling out of urad dhal) and *kadalai* (chickpeas sautéed).

"Send Santhoshi to the Pigeon Meditation camp for Five days of intense meditation," said Pichaiyama.

"Pigeon Meditation Centre?" I said.

"Pigeon Meditation Centre?" said grandma.

'"Pigeon," mom said.

Why are we all repeating things now?

"Pigeon Meditation Centre is run by a Swami blessed by the pigeons," continued P. "I think Santhoshi's betrothal is getting late due to some sin that she committed in her last birth. If, she goes and meditates for five days in this Ashram, she will be blessed and be well."

Mom and grandma looked thoughtful, and I was just flummoxed. I mean seriously me, and meditate. I would probably look somewhat funky in my yoga clothes sitting and meditating something profound.

"How was he blessed by a pigeon?" I asked.

"He was pecked by a pigeon many years ago, but swami lives here now only for few months, he travels most of the time," P said.

"Pigeons are very lucky to have. We always feed pigeons when we see them. If you have pigeons near your house, you should encourage them to live there in many numbers. We learnt when we were young," said mom.

Yes, and you get a whole load of feathers, pooh, and they will be eating all the grains. Seriously, I have noticed that places where pigeons live are extremely wealthy. Like in our grain storage in the paddy fields. Although the pigeons eat up most of the grains and play the merry devil, papa never sends them off.

Pichaiyama droned on about the merits of the swami, and how meditation would help me attract a righteous man. Till that moment, I thought that pigeons were only used to send love letters in the olden times. I suppose, I was a conservative girl and needed the pigeon meditation to get me through this hunt.

The details were taken down swiftly and my mom called the meditation centre. I was indeed a blessed woman; I was admitted to a five-day camp in two days time. Mom and grandma were thrilled and thought it was a sign. I was just going with the flow of things. What else was I to do?

Chapter 20 - Jasmine

We were on our way to the Pigeon Meditation Centre, bright and early. It was a journey of about three hours to reach their retreat, closest to our village. It was idyllically situated on top of a hill. The website looked most beautiful. The chalet type accommodation, with its pristine rooms and the beautiful gardens were an added feature. I was happy on the way; it was just like going away on a nice vacation. I mean of course with that meditation thrown in, certainly a pathway, to become a more calm and collected soul.

Mom was accompanying me to drop me off; she had inquired if she could join too. The centre had said that two members of the same family, joining the retreat at the same time, would be an intrusion on the flow of meditation vibes. Wow, that was a mouthful, but yes, that's what they had said. Mom was generous to let me go first, based on her being a happily married woman. Yes, that is what she said anyways. I was glad to have a change of space; I was rather tired of the same daily routine.

We reached the road towards the retreat. The location was clearly marked by arrow boards, on that lonesome road. There were virtually no vehicles on that road, and then we had to climb the hill. The car could not take the slope; mom and I got off wondering what to do next. Hiking up the hill, was not an option, as it looked like an over grown forest.

Suddenly a little jeep with a picture of a large pigeon arrived as if by a miracle. It was the vehicle used to transport campers to the retreat. A hefty friendly man approached us with his hands clasped in prayer.

"How did you know we were here?" Asked mom in delight.

"The silence of the retreat is disturbed by any vehicle, which approaches the road and we can feel it ma. I am Sundar," he said. "Soon baby, will also feel the same."

Mom was more delighted with this reply and looked at me happily. Who is baby I was wondering, when I realized, the man was referring to me. Oh great, so I will know when a Tsunami is coming up or some disaster is approaching, if I could sense all the movements.

We got into the jeep and were immediately surrounded by the smell of Jasmine Incense. I love the smell of Jasmine but this was terribly intoxicating. For a moment, I felt I was in a Jasmine garden and looked at mom. She looked slightly dazed.

"What is this incense?" she asked.

"An incense made especially for the Pigeon Meditation Centre. They will not sell this incense; it is only for the use of the centre ma," he said.

"Very nice, Very nice," she said.

Suddenly, the jeep did a little lurch, and we were in a cliffhanger position. Mom and I held each other tightly.

"What's happening?" mom whispered.

"No ma, it is bad road, but look at the view!" said Sundar.

We looked out into the hill in fear, and the drop down would surely kill us. What a way to die, the magnificence of nature was abundantly out there. I am sure this is just a preview of my journey to heaven. There were birds flying, trees rich in vegetation, a waterfall flowing freely and oh dear we were going to die.

The jeep took off with more swerving, and we were on a rocky road adventure up the hill. I wanted to rush to the loo, wherever that was.

I could hear mom muttering Lord Krishna be with me. I am sure he heard, cause we approached a drive way. We got off the jeep with a sigh of relief. That was close, I thought. Mom quickly recovered and gushed in delight.

"It is not the incense, the Jasmine flowers," mom said.

118 *Spices Are Sweet*

Indeed the garden; was full of Jasmine Flowers. They looked like some hybrid variety. I have not seen such big flowers. The big signs of "Do Not Pick Flowers," were highlighted in stark bold signs.

"Sundar you think you can get me a small cutting of that flower plant?" Mom mumbled with a waggle of her eyebrows.

"No *maji* we cannot do that kind of thing here. Swami has instructed the flowers cannot be grown anywhere else," he said kindly taking my bag into the ashram.

"Welcome to the Pigeon Meditation Centre. *Namaste,*" said a middle-aged pleasant woman, who was a foreigner in Indian clothes.

"Namaste," said mom and looked at me delightedly.

"I am Anna Karan," she continued looking at us with a smile.

"Like Donna Karan, I buy her underwear always the best," said mom.

I looked at mom in shock, and Anna looked astounded.

"Why don't you come in and register, Santhoshi isn't it?" She said looking at me a bit sternly.

"Yes, I am Santhoshi, this is my mom."

"Anna you must visit us, when you come near to our house," mom gushed in an anglicised accent.

Oh dear lord. Mom was excited on seeing a foreigner and acting weird. Anna just ignored her and strode past purposefully. I rushed into a lovely area, which had quite a number of people seated and were in line registering.

"Ma, what are you doing?" I hissed.

"Being friendly to the foreigner in our land. She can have a taste of our culture," mom replied.

"I don't think she is interested. What are you talking mom, Dona Karan underwear?" I replied with my eyebrows arched up.

"I want her to know that we also wear foreign things, I think I saw this name somewhere. Your mother she remembers so

DD 119

many details. What other way to become close friends with a woman, than to discuss underwear," mom continued. "Let me call Papa," she said taking out her mobile.

Seriously, I have no idea, why my mother was talking about underwear to a person, we just met and calling my father to update him on the situation. Well, papa was more sensible than she was and hopefully would talk some sense to mom, before things get out of hand here.

"Sorry madam we don't receive signals in here," rushed an Indian woman with a little nametag of assistant on her.

"Oh," said mom.

"No mobiles allowed, you can handover your mobile, wallet, everything, to your mother. She can bring it, when she comes to pick you," she said, handing over a sizeable docket sort of thing to me.

Oh, it did say I wouldn't be allowed to bring any personal effects, except my clothes. I guess, I had not paid attention to it very carefully. I think to me the mobile; laptop and iPod were personal effects.

I opened the docket, it had a head spinning set of rules, which clearly specified that I could not bring any entertainment gadgets. I looked at mom who looked delirious and happy with the setup.

I looked at the other participants; 10 women that ranged from middle age to elderly. There was just one other girl, who looked like my age. She was wearing a trendy trouser with a lovely top and a cute hat on her head. She was reading the docket intently. The other women had not even opened the docket; they were regulars surely.

"Mom I won't be able to talk to you for five days," I said.

"Anna is here to look after you, and jasmine flowers are here for you to smell. No electronic gadget, very good for you. You must meditate seriously, and you will be very happy!" she said smiling.

"Anna Anna," called out mom to the fair woman.

120 *Spices Are Sweet*

Maybe I was better off not talking to mom for five days. Anna looked slightly irritated and came towards us.

"Madam you should be on your way. It's time to close the doors and start the programme. Your daughter will be as happy as her name is.," said Anna with a stiff smile.

"I told her that you will look after her Anna. Just keep an eye on her; she is very much upset these days, without this marriage working. We saw many boys," mom ranted.

"Yes Madam. Thank you bye." Anna cut her short. "Give your personal effects to your mother," and she walked off.

"See Santhoshi, Anna will give you special treatment. You saw this is how we have to get people to work for us being charming, like me."

I shook my head, if mom thought she was charming and that Anna was going to treat me like a VIP. The world will inevitably end at this point. After all this drama, I am sure I will be better off lying low.

"Tell grandma I will miss her and Papa that I am going to be ok," I said touching my mom's feet for blessings.

I don't know what made me do that. I hardly fall at her feet, which is the farthest sort of blessing, you get from your parents. Mom pulled me up and held me close. She never was the hugging type, so I was glad to be held in her warmth.

"The next time you fall at my feet will be with your husband," She said tearfully.

"Bye Anna Girl." waving towards Anna.

Mom walked off, without looking at me wiping her eyes, Sundar rushed out after her, I felt like crying. The woman with the assistant badge appeared by my side, with a set of applications. It was like a twenty page one and I felt tired before starting on it. The details were taken over swiftly, and my mom left the meditation centre.

I opened the docket, which ran into pages. I felt terribly tired and could not be bothered to read it. The assistant appeared by my side, as if reading my mind.

DD 121

"Please, sign here agreeing to the contract child," she smiled benevolently, pointing to the dotted space.

I signed it quickly and noticed the other women handing their contracts in. The funky girl was still reading the pages intently, and Anna was talking to her in whispers. They seemed to be having an argument of some sort. As if sensing, Anna turned and waved smilingly, and pointed the girl towards a room marked private. The funky girl turned and looked at me unsmilingly, and followed Anna.

The silent Assistant was by my side, I wonder how she moves, and I felt so tired.

"I will show you the room," she said smiling.

I followed her out of the area and came to a vast room, which had rooms like structure on the sides. The strange thing was there was a high compound wall covering the whole area. You were on the top of a hill but you could not see any nature. I stopped in shock at the way it was. The assistant smiled at me and pointed to an area, which looked like the garden. There were flocks of large Pigeons walking around. I approached the birds, and the strange thing, was they did not fly away, but carried on with their own thing, ignoring me. There were little benches on the sides but it was pointless as there was no sense sitting on a bench and looking at a bleak dark wall. It was almost as if they did not want anyone to see nature or anything beautiful.

"Come I will show you the room," the assistant prodded me.

I shook my head in agreement and followed her. She took me into a large room, which had several beds; it reminded me of a general ward in a hospital. She quickly pointed to the bed number three and proceeded to open out the curtains separating the beds. The bed looked anything but comfortable with no pillows; the curtains were dull and dreary. Grey was the colour theme. This was not what I had seen on the website. My little hold- all was kept by the bedside.

"Bathroom," she pointed in the general direction of the other end of the room. "You can rest now; we will ring the bell for Tea."

I sat on the hard bed and burst out into tears.

Chapter 21 - Cloves

I woke up to the sound of a bell ringing. The pooja bell for prayers, I thought. I woke up groggily, and my whole body ached, I could not quite figure out where I was. I looked around in confusion. I was in a grey dungeon.

"Arghh," I screamed.

The assistant woman was by the curtain in a minute.

"You are disturbing the peace of the mediation centre, SHHH," she whispered with a finger on her lips, indicating me to shut up.

The nightmare had not ended; I was playing the main role in it. I remember crying and must have dozed off for a bit. My bladder was ready to burst. I immediately rushed to the toilet. The toilet was real old and wet. I wanted to cry some more, but had to rush in and use it. I could hear the other prisoners getting ready in the curtained spaces.

I came out splashing some water on my face. Two middle-aged women were moving out of their curtain space, they did not nod their head or seem to notice me. I rushed into the cubicle space and opened the bag, to find that it was a mess inside. There was no makeup, deodorant or hairbrush. Only three sets of clothes and underwear were in there. Half the bag was empty. My hair was a mess, and I was totally unkempt.

Opening the curtain and walking out Ms. Silent mover was there standing.

"I can't find my comb."

"You don't beautify yourself in the centre. We check the bag and take out unnecessary stuff out. It is kept safely in our office room. Just do this," she replied.

She took her palm and patted her hair, which was already, in place. Strangely, I doubted that she did that elaborate bun on her head patting it like that. She proceeded to come and pat my hair; at which I shrieked in alarm and said no. Last thing, I needed was a strange woman patting my head into place.

"Hurry up then. Or no Tea for you," she barked.

Damn it, I would do anything for a cup of tea. I heard a cough and turned to see Ms. Funky watching me. Her hair looked neatly in place; she had it short up to her ears. I dislike people who have hair, which stays in place even when there is a tornado.

"They don't give you any of your personal possessions, which includes your make up kit. Did you not read the contract? You have to use their bathing powder to bathe, and some gunk to wash your hair. No combing of your hair. Nothing," she said.

The look of alarm in my face was obvious.

"You did not read it did you? Seriously, what kind of an idiot are you signing yourself up without reading," she said.

I turned and stomped off in anger and walked straight towards a white wall. I turned around to see Ms. Funky and the assistant watch me in disbelief. I quickly noticed that all the women were assembled at the exact opposite side holding cups of Tea. There was silence; except for the pigeons. I walked towards the table and saw three metal cups with a brownish liquid with some leaves floating on it. It looked most disgusting, like the cough medicine grandma would make as a home remedy.

I took one sip and felt like throwing up; it was some cheap tea with some leaves in it. I kept it aside and saw Ms. Funky look into her cup and keep it away. There was a faint sound of rumbling; Ms. Funky looked at me pointedly. I was hungry and my stomach was dancing.

I noticed a small plate with cloves. I took a few and started munching on them, to keep my teeth clean and fresh. I was so hungry and tired the spicy clove was making my mouth burn.

"Welcome again to the Pigeon Meditation," announced Anna, standing in the middle of the courtyard.

124 *Spices Are Sweet*

"Quick re-cap of our rules here, you cannot talk to anyone else and should practice the art of being silent. The voyage to self-discovery starts here. Your meditation will soon follow the path in the right time. Please enter the Meditation Cave over here, and sit at the places allocated to you. Your bed number is your place number," she said.

"No eating when I am talking!" Anna said looking at me.

Oh well munching on a few cloves is not like eating a full meal.

I noticed that all the women looked untidy and dishevelled, except the people at the Centre. The Centre people looked decent and neat. The women were all moving towards the small garden area, where the pigeons were still strutting around. The area did indeed lead into a small cave area, which was not a cave. It was a spacious room, with little carpets, strewn with numbers. There were many helpers around the hall. Another Indian woman was seated at the small raised platform.

Ms. Assistant crept in beside me and pointed my place. I sat in between two old aunties who did not make any eye contact with me.

"*Namaste*. My name is Sheila. Today we will start out meditation by listening to the song by Pigeon Swami. Listen to the song, breathe deeply and start thinking," she concluded.

The little platform had a white screen and was alive with a hazy figure in white, in between many pigeons started to sing. The projector was playing some video clip. I freaked out; it was some real inferior quality singing. The man was worse than I was in that department, and he was singing in a language, which I did not understand. It was freaking me out. Very unbearable, I wanted to scream in hunger and in despair of this moment.

I think someone heard me, because I heard sniffling sounds. I turned around in surprise to watch the women next to me crying. Everyone was crying, and for a second time in a short spell, I burst out into tears. I mean surely, this was terrible; we must all cry and protest to stop this nonsense. I started crying again, I want to go home.

The swami was getting particularly high in pitch, and my ears were paining. The swami's figure became extremely clear, and there stood a man, who looked like a villain in a bad Indian movie. I was shocked, I mean there were distant photos of him on the website, but a close up of his video, almost gave me a heart attack. He looked evil.

Thankfully, the video clipping was over, with a giant pigeon in the end. I had stopped crying by this time, the rest of the party was also recovering, and keeping their eyes closed. I could hear one of the assistants admonishing Ms. Funky for not participating. I strained my ears, but could not hear what her reply was.

"Meditation is joy and sorrow you will make the hard journey and find yourself in paradise," said Sheila.

I was exceedingly tired and nodded off, while she was droning on about something or the other. I need to get the hell out of here, I thought.

Thud I had hit the floor. In the combined effort, of sitting and pretending to meditate, I had nodded off to sleep. My head almost hit the floor. The assistant had put a pillow to stop me from breaking my brain open. The rest of the gang was deep in meditation or sleep. I was lying there with my head on a pillow, with the assistant trying to pull me up. I saw Funky Girl trying hard not to laugh at me. I immediately sat up and pretended to close my eyes.

"Concentrate," whispered the assistant before moving off.

I wish I had read the rules and what was happening around. I think, I mistook this Spartan life for a retreat in the spa. I saw the pictures and assumed it's a holiday with nature and now I was at some sort of weirdo chanting and a not so happening place. My back was aching and my thighs felt as if two large cannon balls were tied to them. My whole body was hurting like hell, I am sure I was going to become sick now. I suddenly felt anger towards my mom for leaving me here; she should have checked the room at least. The need to get out of the '*Place*,' was increasing by the minute. I was distressed. The assistant was watching me closely from the sides.

"Trapped is the word that you should meditate on, you will feel trapped. Come out of it," said Sheila looking straight at me.

126 *Spices Are Sweet*

I was freaked out and closed my eyes shut. How could she read me? I had to open my eyes in fear of falling again and making a fool of myself. I have no idea how long we sat there, but it was one of the longest periods of my life. The clang of the bell was a welcome relief. I got up and followed the women out.

Dinner was set out in the courtyard; I heard my stomach grumble. The women had formed an instant queue and were serving food on to their plates. I stood at the end of the queue and Funky girl joined right after. She giggled when she passed me; I chose to ignore that. As, I approached the table it was obvious that it was not a five course meal that I was going to get tonight. There was a hard roti and watery dhal, with some old chilli and onion floating on it. The rice was a mixture of wild country rice and some suspicious gunk. I took one roti and a little of the other stuff.

"The food at this Centre is cooked with secret recipes from the swami himself," announced Sheila.

Well! The man was no Adele in Singing, and his cooking skills were certainly not Antony. I sat on a wooden bench holding the plate; funky girl came and sat next to me. I looked at her ready to stare her to death. She just looked at me, with no expression and sat taking a small piece of roti.

I took a piece into my mouth and spat it out, there was no salt, and it was some strange tasting food. I closed my eyes and took a deep breath as taught in yoga. The heady fragrance of Jasmine filled my lungs quickly. I took more gulps and it was relaxing me. Maybe I had committed some sin in my previous birth and this was a way of paying amends to it. I took the plate, and threw the meal into the garbage and washed my hands.

"You should not waste precious food. So you don't get your cup of milk," whispered the assistant and walked off.

The rest of the assembled women were eating slowly and thoughtfully. Ms. Funky was watching me, and her plate was empty. I wondered how she had eaten that up, even a small amount.

I knew I was defeated spiritually, after a few hours in this place, I was depressed and ready to throw in the towel.

Chapter 22 - Chocolate

I was seated inside a comfortable room; awaiting the departure. After the scrumptious dinner, I rushed into the room and closed up my bag. Ms. Assistant followed me in and looked at the bag.

"You must meet Sheilaji and tell her that you want to leave. Go slowly towards the arrival area. We don't want the other ladies upset with your departure," she whispered.

Well, the woman could mind read. I was convinced that the women, would not be bothered if I stayed or buggered off from the place. Ms. Funky was watching me, as I walked off; I gave her a look of triumph. Well, I shouldn't have, but I stuck my tongue out at her, before walking into the reception area. The woman at the receptionist showed me into a room. I was waiting there for a long time, I have no idea how long, but it must have been quite long. There were no clocks anywhere, and I had no watch on me.

The room had real comfy antique furniture and beautiful curtains. There was an apple Mac on the table, and the refreshing breeze from the air conditioner was a welcome relief. Maybe, I should immediately turn on the laptop that was facing the opposite direction and use it to check my email. Well, it would be rude, if I were caught, so I decided to wait. I realized that the bed, I had been allocated had no fans or even a window for ventilation. There was the shrill ringing of the landline phone, outside somewhere. There was no phone inside this room.

I saw a small door with a bathroom and decided to use it. I opened the door and nearly balked, the toilet was of five star hotel standards. With the works, complete with candlelights. I

128 *Spices Are Sweet*

went in and refreshed myself and used the face wash they had. I walked out, and Sheilaji was on the chair.

"*Namaste* Santhoshi. It's always natural that you feel the need to go home on the first day," she said smilingly.

"I feel sick, I don't think I read the contract well and I miss my parents," I replied truthfully.

"I was just on the phone with your mother; she called to say that she has reached home. The path to finding inner peace is a long one. But, it takes less time, than that of finding you a husband."

Uhm, what the heck was she talking about? As if, she could read me.

"Your mom told us about your turbulent journey in finding a soul mate. Your journey is at the departure lounge of this Pigeon Centre. At the end, you will find joy," she continued.

At the end of this, I might die of starvation.

"You are not happy with the meals I hear? A delicious meal full of fat, would only make your mind fluffy. The special meal prepared with care from '*Swamis Recipe*' will cleanse your system and prepare your mind to be pure," she said.

"I feel terribly ill Sheila ji," I whimpered and stifled some sobs.

I want to, need to get out of here.

"Your mom will be so disappointed if you leave from here early. You will let down yourself, your family and everyone. It is only four more nights. Can you give up something so early?" she questioned.

The assistant woman appeared with a glass of something, I shook my head that I don't want it. The woman just placed it in front of me. It looked like a chocolate milk shake with chocolate sauce on it. Then again, I could be hallucinating and it could be pigeon droppings. Oh, lord! What was I thinking?

"Have your milkshake child; I am giving this specially to you to adjust with staying. We won't be providing this every day. Also, you have disappointed Swami by not eating," she admonished.

I am totally shameless; I devoured the milkshake, which was

yummy. It was certainly one of the best milk shakes I have had; I could taste some nutella and Hershey's chocolate syrup dripping. The sugar rush was going right to my head, and I was happy. This certainly was not one of the pigeon's masterpieces.

The assistant appeared silent by my side. Oh, ok, so that's it. I am given a milk shake, and I have to stay?

"Go have a digestive medicine that everyone else is given in the Centre, to cleanse the system and go to bed. *Namaste*." She said looking at her computer.

I wanted to argue with her about my departure, except it would have seemed frightfully rude to do that after drinking all that milkshake. Therefore, I walked out with the assistant.

"You can't even think of leaving in the night like that. The hill is full of snakes," said the assistant slowly.

Snakes? I felt the fear in the pit of my stomach. I looked at her in horror. She gave me a tiny, translucent pill and a glass of water. I looked at the pill in the shape of a tiny marble. The woman was watching me like a hawk. Ms. Funky appeared from nowhere, and the assistant looked annoyed.

"I want water," Ms. Funky said.

"No water now, it is lights out. How did you come out like this? Where is your care-taker?" the assistant was angry now.

"I want water now," Ms. Funky repeated.

"Wait till I come back and drink the pill in front of me." The assistant said going inside.

"Throw the pill out," Ms. Funky said.

I stood there dumbstruck. She shoved me to make a point. I could see my assistant coming out with a glass of water and another burly woman coming towards us.

I threw the pill behind and a pigeon from nowhere appeared, and ate it from the floor.

"No coming out after lights out. I was right there how did you slip out?" inquired the burly woman, who must be Flunky's assistant.

130 *Spices Are Sweet*

"Water," Funky said.

"Where is the pill?" asked my assistant.

I opened my mouth out and showed her.

"You had chocolate?" Ms. Funky questioned.

My assistant was prodding me to move towards the sleeping area and signalling us to cut the conversation. I took a sip of my water and was shocked that it tasted strange. There was a muddy and herbal blend of a taste. The tinge was so slight; it might have been my imagination.

"I don't know why they tax us with these young liberal types," said the burly one to my assistant in Hindi.

She had assumed I do not know Hindi. Only if she had realized, how fluent I was in Hindi, after watching the TV serials. My assistant did not reply and just kept walking. I was branded, a liberal for wanting to leave early, I felt decidedly euphoric. Maybe it was all that sugar rush. I don't know what they put into the milk shake but my stomach was full.

All the curtains were drawn and I could hear the gentle snoring of someone. I went near my bed and turned around to see my curtain was drawn. I was alone; I lay down on the bed, realizing I had not brushed my teeth. The thought of the bathroom gave me the creeps. I lay there in silent thought. I could hear Ms. Funky and the Burly woman come in and walk somewhere away.

I was awake for a long time, listening to the frogs croaking in some nearby pond. I got a vision of the poor froggies being eaten up by bulky anaconda snakes. I opened my eyes and sat up with a fear. The woman told me there are snakes around the hills. I have no way to escape from the place.

I felt beads of perspiration on my forehead and neck. I could not sleep now and must have been awake for a long time sitting on my bed. The curtain swished quickly, and Ms. Funky was near my bed. Oh my god, I was going to be molested.

"Shh," She signalled telling me to follow her.

I was just waiting petrified with fear on the bed. Where is she calling me to? She turned and had an exasperated look on her

DD 131

face. She signalled to hurry and remain silent. Well I had to go find out, and if she did molest me, I could scream the place down.

I followed her through the curtains to the far end of the corridor. We passed three sleeping women who were knocked out and snoring. I giggled at one, who had her mouth wide open. Ms. Funky gave me a look of warning. We passed one who was muttering in her sleep. We passed an empty bed in the middle, which was her bed. We passed more empty beds and were in the last room. She told me to sit down and did a quick check, opening the curtain and under the bed.

"I am Rupa," she gave her hand out.

I shook it dumbly; I wonder what Rupa *aka* Ms. Funky had in mind for me.

"You are Santhoshi. Your mom screamed your name a couple of times," she said with a smile.

I just sat there with no idea of what was going to happen next. Rupa spoke quietly, but earnestly. I was listening with my mouth open wide. She was a newspaper reporter, who had come on a special mission, to find out what actually was happening in the Centre. Rupa took out a granola bar and offered me half.

"How did you get a granola bar? I don't want it. I had a milkshake in Sheila's office."

"Milkshake? They gave you a milk shake to make sure you stay on course. That's good information. You are my assistant for this investigation," Rupa said.

I told her the milkshake saga and Sheila's elegant room, the bit about the snakes. Rupa explained how she had a false bottom in her bag, filled with water and snacks. The pill was some sort of sleeping pill, since everyone else was knocked out. She felt the water was mixed with something and had already managed to nick some in a little bottle. She had not eaten or touched anything. I pointed out that in five days, she would not be able to pull it off. Rupa agreed that they were somewhat suspicious of her, since she arrived.

The contract does not accept any media persons within. She

132 *Spices Are Sweet*

felt the pigeons were drugged, and the air was sprayed with some sort of drug. It was a cult movement, which just brought together ordinary people and turned them into fanatics.

"We are always watched and followed at all time; they have assigned one assistant to each member. These old aunties here are addicted to this place. Smell yourself." Rupa ordered.

I smelt my skin, the smell of jasmine and something else on me. I smelt some strands of my hair, and I could smell the same. The air here was filled with some kind of intoxicating fragrance.

"This is dangerous Rupa. What if you get caught?" I said.

"They are running a cult but, I don't think they are murderers," said Rupa with a smile.

I looked at her quizzically. I was in the middle of a cult, with snakes down the hill, a news investigator as a friend, and some bribe chocolate milkshake inside my stomach. Life does not get more exciting than this.

Chapter 23 - Pepper

The next morning dawned bleak and early. Very early, I had hardly gotten any sleep and the moment I was asleep, the bell rang. It was dark. Surely, it must be around four a.m. or something. I was dis-oriented. I peeped out and saw a queue for the bathroom. There was only one woman, a new one outside my curtain. She was walking around, waking up the aunties who were still in sleepy land. I saw Rupa come out of her little room. I did not make eye contact, as she had instructed me not to.

Some of the women were lining up to leave the area. I decided to join them to see what exactly this leads up to. So, we walked into the open court- yard, and the assistant just instructed us to walk around. Sheilaji or Anna was not there. Those lazy cows must be sleeping well. We were walking around, and I could see the older women were finding it hard to walk. What with hardly any food in their system and some drug in as well, they were physically not in a condition for this health walk. I slowed down my pace, and put on a deadpan expression. I could see Rupa in the corner of my eye.

"Meditation hall," said the assistant.

Oh no! I cannot go there and watch the swamis little dabble with singing. Really, maybe I should have taken that pill and been drugged out instead. Anything was better than listening to him crooning. The hall was dimly lit, and we took our places. Everyone just sat there still with their eyes closed. Thank god, there was no video for the morning session. I shall just close my eyes and sit still.

I was in a daze, when I woke up. Oh dear. I must have fallen asleep. I opened my eyes to see that there was no one around

134 *Spices Are Sweet*

me. Where had they disappeared to? I got up and rushed out to the courtyard. The usual assistant came up to me and did a slight nod. The others were all assembled for breakfast. Rupa was trying hard not to laugh, I could see. She must have noticed that I had a siesta in the morning.

I looked at the pigeons; they were walking around as if sleep walking. Suddenly, it was extremely obvious, I saw one particular pigeon that could barely walk, the poor bird was just standing, and the other birds were pushing past.

"Have your breakfast," said the assistant.

"The bird is ill," I said pointing at the pigeon.

The assistant just looked over and did nothing; she was obviously waiting for me to come to the breakfast buffet. I was terribly thirsty and hungry. I had to check the bird out. So, I walked up and bent over near the bird. The pigeon was out there with the fairies. As if by miracle, Anna had arrived at the scene.

"*Namaste* Santhoshi. We hear great things about your meditation, which ran over time today. Now you are with the pigeons, without going for breakfast. The meditation is working wonders on you my dear," Anna preached with a look of approval.

"This bird is ill. She needs help immediately. Could you arrange something," I pleaded.

Anna looked over at the bird, and she frowned. She barked orders at the assistant to take the bird out.

"Join the breakfast my dear." Anna addressed me.

I got up and saw Rupa watching me, I took one look at her face, and I knew. This was the pigeon that had eaten up the pill; I threw off last night. The bird had been overdosed on the drug. I moved towards the breakfast buffet. I had to have water, my throat was parched and my tongue was dry. I was scared to take a sip of the water here. I saw water glasses and plain tea glasses. Maybe tea was a safer bet, so I took a sip of the horrid concoction. Breakfast was some chickpeas boiled, unsalted, and a few beaten up bananas. There was a peppershaker left to one side, which no one was taking. The point was lost, why they had left only pepper.

I took a small amount of chickpeas, unsalted and one banana. I remembered the delicious breakfast at home. This certainly was turning out into a weight loss trip. If I keep up at this rate, I am certainly going to lose some weight. The other members were eating the chickpeas and bananas.

"Please have a short rest and refresh yourselves, the bell will ring at 9.30 a.m. for the morning session," announced Anna.

The assistants were passing small sachets of powders. It was labelled bathing powder and looked like some sand in a clear packet. I moved towards the room area.

"Santhoshi, can I have a word with you?" announced Anna.

Oh dear! She knows about the midnight tryst. I wonder what kind of damage this will bring about. Maybe I have to sleep with the pigeons or something. I walked towards Anna. The others had all walked back to their cell; oops room by now.

"You know why I have called you?" she inquired.

I did the head-nodding thing, which did not respond in the positive or negative.

"You must have a guess?" she continued.

"I am sorry Annaji, I don't..." I started.

"Why are you sorry, you are meditating beyond your age? You observed the pigeon that was dying of old age. You are doing wonderfully. Your mom will be so proud of you. She has been phoning continuously. We told her how well you were doing, she was insistent that you call. I had a hard time convincing her that it is not possible." She said with a smile.

I just nodded mutely.

"You will be blessed by swami, you are practicing your silent stance even now," she gushed.

I was practicing my silence, because I was just about to walk into the trap, and provide a tell-all of the investigation.

"We have a small problem that we need help with. You are the chosen one for this. There is a young woman here on the course, Ms. Rupa. You would have noticed her very bright clothes. She

136 *Spices Are Sweet*

does not seem to have any interest in the meditation. She is of trouble. You have to keep an eye on her," finished Anna.

I just nodded like a fool for the nth time this morning. I wonder what makes people confide in me. Must be my innocent look, or my bright eyes.

"We knew we could trust you. In the night, you can come, see me, and report anything that Rupa does. We can get you a nice chocolate pie," she smiled.

I was shocked; the woman thought, she could buy me with a piece of chocolate pie. Well I will show her who I was. I will eat the pie and double cross her. I just nodded saintly, or so I thought and did a bow with a prayer. Anna was somewhat taken aback with my abrupt ending to the chocolate pie bribe, and she did the same.

I walked back to the room and could hear the shower turned on, someone was in the shower. I was wondering how to avoid the bathing with the powder. Maybe I can just wash my face and take a bath in the evening. I lay down on the bed and was asleep instantly.

I don't know how long I was asleep for, but was woken up by my mother's voice.

"Let me in you silly girl," she was screaming.

I woke up and shook my head, I must be dreaming. There was some trouble and I could hear people moving around. I walked out of the room. I noticed that some of the aunties and Rupa were assembled in the entrance. It was obvious most of them had decided to skip on hygiene and were not having a bath in the morning. The crumpled clothes of yesterday hung around their bodies.

"Santhoshi, Santhoshi," screamed my mom.

Oh god, mom was here. I ran out, and there was mom, held behind by two assistants.

"Mom." I screamed and ran towards her.

"Oh my child, they did not let me speak to you, and your uncle was angry that I had left you behind. Then papa was also upset.

I had to come back. Sundar tried to stop me come up the hill," she was on a roll holding me close.

"Please, everyone just go back into the rooms," announced Anna in a voice that could melt ice.

I looked at her, and she looked fearfully angry. Sheilaji and the assistants were also looking unhappy behind her.

"Come we are going home," said my mom.

"That sounds the best thing I have heard in the past twenty four hours mom," I replied.

The rest of the aunties had left, and Rupa was in an argument with the assistant.

"I will get my bag mom," I said.

"I will get your bag, don't step inside," barked Anna.

"You want a lift?" I asked Rupa.

I was not leaving her behind in this strange place. Rupa looked at me seriously; there was a hushed silence except for mom sobbing. Rupa broke into a smile and nodded.

"You both know each other?" Spat out Sheila and Anna in unison.

The assistant came out with both our bags and we followed mom out.

"These girls come here because they are bored. They can't do meditation for five days, how will they ever find a man," mumbled the assistant. "Shut up," yelled mom and thumped her with her handbag.

"We have a procedure for leaving. You have to sign another set of documents," said Anna.

"We are not signing," replied Rupa.

"Rupa, you have been trouble from the day you arrived. We suggest you sign the final Non-Disclosure Agreement. You agreed to sign it on the first day," Anna said.

"Let us leave now quickly, you both look like you have not eaten for days," said mom tearing.

138 *Spices Are Sweet*

"We don't want to make it difficult, you have to sign the forms," said Sheila.

"I knew it, what is this nonsense sign the form, sign the form?" asked mom.

"We cannot allow you to leave the place if you don't sign the form. The pigeon retreat is not for people like you, who come and don't stay for the entire course," explained Sheila.

"We will keep your valuables Rupa if you are not going to sign."

"Ok get the forms we will sign," replied mom.

"No, I don't want to sign," said Rupa.

"You can take your daughter and leave madam, we will talk to Rupa," replied Anna.

"I am not leaving Rupa behind," I said opening my mouth after a short spell of silence.

A man walked out of the room as if by magic.

"I am the lawyer of the Pigeon retreat. I believe that there is a problem in signing the non-disclosure," he said with a smile.

In the next ten minutes, he mentioned many rules and regulations. Mom was whispering, asking if I was ok and that she is sorry. I was half-heartedly listening to the lawyer and nodding to mom. It seemed Rupa's refusal to sign the documents; they could sue her. She had, well both of us had signed something to that effect.

"Child I am like your mother, please sign, and we can all go home," said mom.

So that was sorted out .We signed a bunch of forms, which essentially said we were not to violate and talk about the meditation camp. It ran into many pages.

Chapter 24 – Cinnamon

Finally, we were on our way home, with mom sobbing her heart out. Rupa had given her a re-cap of her suspicions. She had also called her home and told them that she was on her way.

"So when will your story come out?" I asked Rupa.

"It's tricky; we have signed legal documents, so I might not be able to write it. Thank you, for not leaving me behind. What made you ask me? I would have thought you would have left the minute you saw your mom," she said.

"Well, I could not forget and leave you behind, I heard you arguing with the assistant," I giggled.

We burst out laughing.

"I will track down Pichaiyma and fire her for sure," said mom in the midst of her sobbing.

"No ma, I think it was our mistake, we should have read the rules. Checked the rooms and found out before jumping into it," I said.

"Papa is going to kill me," said mom with a look of fear in her eyes.

We were passing the end of the hill and I saw the video camera attached in the plants. I showed the same to Rupa. I wanted to stick out my tongue and make a face, but something stopped me.

"I will take off at the bus station in town and take a bus back to my city," Rupa said.

"Let's eat first and then we will drop you," announced mom recovering quickly.

140 *Spices Are Sweet*

We had a lovely meal at a roadside restaurant, rice and three kinds of vegetables. Rupa and I could not eat much, but we agreed that it was scrumptious. I drank two bottles of water. I caught myself in the mirror near the hand wash. I looked a hippie, with crushed clothes, unkempt hair and downright dirty. We dropped Rupa near a bus stand, and I hugged her goodbye, with a promise to keep in touch. I fell asleep after that all the way home. I had dreams of the Pigeon who was ill, flying towards me. It was strange; I was singing but in that high pitched terrible tone. The dream had turned into a nightmare.

I came home to the welcome committee of my uncles and aunts and some of the older cousins. Everyone asked several questions, I was so tired. Grandma looked at me guiltily.

"Your uncle said that it was not a good meditation place. They take away young people, and they never come back," she whispered.

"I am sorry, your mother is a silly woman," said papa looking at me.

"It's not her fault. I really cannot say much about it. It was a different experience. I need to shower and sleep," I said.

"You have to eat before your sleep, you have lost so much weight," said grandma with a soft sob.

Mother was holding court, giving her story how she saved me and all the young girls there. The way she was telling the story, I wondered where I came into the picture. Mom was the superwoman of the day.

Later, that night I was on the rooftop counting stars. These few months flashed by like a slide show. I had met many new people and characters. The strangest of all, was the time at the retreat. I took a few strands of my hair, and the smell was still there. I had used shampoo and conditioner to wash my hair but still the Jasmine smell from the retreat remained.

"Oh oooh or," said someone.

It was a strange sound, I turned around and there on the ledge of the wall there was a fat pigeon. The bird was looking at me. I felt a chill in my heart; it was for a moment. I went close and the bird was still there, it did not fly away in fear. I touched it lightly, and she hopped onto my arm. I looked at her and knew that she was the one who had eaten the pill. I had goose bumps. I ran downstairs and got some raw rice, mom and grandma were glued on the TV. When I got back to the roof, the pigeon was still there; I fed her some rice.

When I went to bed that night, I felt a sense of calm in my heart. I called Maya, who was rocking around in laughter at the whole episode. She was convinced that the pigeon was not the same, but some other bird, who knew that I was a cuckoo, meaning I was crazy. I hung up and wondered whom I could tell this. Rupa, I called her, she was extremely quiet listening to my escapade.

"You think I am mad don't you?" I asked her.

"I know it's the same bird Santhoshi," Rupa replied and she burst out crying.

I was horrified and kept asking her what happened. Rupa was not crying in despair but in joy. She had a scholarship to study journalism in the States.

"Congratulations. Why are you crying?" I asked in confusion.

"There were five thousand candidates who applied. Many were much better than I. I got it, and I believe it has something to do with the retreat," she said.

"Oh," I said slowly. "You think we should have stayed?"

"No, I think we were meant to stay there only for a night. I am not going back there. I am not going to talk about it either," Rupa said slowly.

"I can still smell the Jasmine in my hair," I said.

"Me too," replied Rupa.

"What about the pills? What about the mind games with the food? What about Anna and Sheila talking crap all the time. The swami who sang terribly," I said.

"It does not make sense; I came to write a story about the place. I am not going to do it now. I don't have answers for your questions or mine, really," she replied.

142 *Spices Are Sweet*

I wished her luck and hung up. It was a strange feeling; last night I had been at the Centre. Today, I had a bird, which had followed me hundreds of miles to be here.

Everyone at home was fascinated with the Pigeon who had come to visit. They joked with me that I had hidden and brought one home as a pet. Mom tried to take credit that she in fact, had found the bird as a pet for me. I just smiled and nodded, never once mentioning that she was from the retreat.

The pigeon stayed on for the next month. My MBA exam was coming up in Chennai and I was busy studying. Life was going on at the slow pace; I was cooking extraordinarily well. All the grandmothers' recipes were being cooked, photographed and blogged by me. In the one month, I started blogging the recipes; I had seven hundred followers on my blog Cinnamon. The numbers kept growing at a steady pace. I was interviewed by a leading magazine. Mom was thrilled, brought the magazine, and sent it to all the relatives.

Rupa called me from states, "I hear Congratulations are in order."

"How are you? The strangest thing happened. Wait, how did you know?" I stopped.

"The pigeon told me," she said.

I was silent for a moment and heard Rupa laugh.

"My sister had seen your interview, and she told me to check out this blog which has easy recipes. I saw the link with your interview and it clicked. I was so happy. I had to call you. I love the photographs and your blog is amazing," Rupa said.

"The pigeon is still here Rupa," I said.

"Yes and your hair still smell of Jasmines," she finished

I had to hang up abruptly; it was Lord Krishna's birthday, a religious festival that involved making plenty of food. The new chef in the house, yours truly, was assigned the task. I had to make sweets and savouries. The prayer room was cleaned and decorated. Little motifs of a pair of legs were drawn with a mix made of flour and water. The little footprint motifs would lead from the entrance to the prayer room. It marked that the Lord would follow the footsteps and try out the feast laid out for him. I had loved the whole story and the rituals associated with it, since childhood.

I had finished making the sweet *laddu* and savoury *seedai* (little balls of rice flour, coconut and ghee). Mom complimented that they were as good as hers. I had to finish drawing the footsteps before bathing to perform the prayers. I remembered the last time we had a powerful prayer and Pichaiyma's arrival. I smiled to myself, the pigeon named Jasmine, was content on our rooftop.

I was drawing the footsteps in our living room, which was leading towards the prayer room. I could hear some chattering. I looked up to see my aunt, two women and a youngish man in the living room.

"Very good Santhoshi, you have drawn almost as well as me," my aunt said.

Women have a sense of comparing themselves. If you can do it, I can do it better.

"She has drawn it better than I can," said the visitor. .

"Hello, please take a seat, I will call my mother," I said.

"You are famous for your cooking," said the woman number two.

The young man was dishevelled and dirty. He looked as if he had run a marathon in the mud. Mom appeared with my grandma, welcomed them, and took them in.

"Hi, excuse my messy appearance. I am Santhosh," he said.

"I am Santoshi," I said with a smile.

"We have similar names. How strange? I was helping out in the paddy field, and my mom just dragged me here. She said urgent, if you don't come I will have a heart attack," he continued.

"Sounds like my mom, are you a farmer?" I asked surprised.

"Yes farmer at heart, stockbroker at work. Here on vacation and helping out in the fields," he said. "Don't get me wrong, but you have some batter on your forehead," he said.

144 *Spices Are Sweet*

I rushed inside, where the women chattered to a dozen. I checked myself in the guest room mirror. I was totally a mess, my hair was unkempt and a whopping streak was on my forehead. I washed my face and moved towards the living room.

"This is my daughter Santhoshi, great chef, she even does recipes on the computer, in magazines, and the newspapers." "Yes we saw the magazine you sent us," replied the woman.

"Can I get you some coffee or tea?" I asked generally.

"No, they just came to say hello. They are leaving now," rushed my aunt.

"Yes we must all perform our prayers," replied the woman.

Then the women all trooped into the living room with mom. Strange that mom did not offer them anything.

"Meet Santhoshi," said my aunt to Santhosh.

He looked at me and said, "HI".

I replied "Hi!"

"You see Santhosh has been unlucky with a bride search for the past year, so we thought if you could meet just for a minute. It will cancel out the bad luck for both of you," said my aunt.

I looked in horror and saw that Santhosh had no clue about it either. Mom was happily waving bye to them. They all trooped out saying bye and Santhosh turned and did a little wave, mouthed sorry and shrugged his shoulder. I did not respond. Seriously, mom is unbearable at times. I am sure this had to do with the fact that papa and grandma had gone to Chennai for a week. I decided not to question mom and went on with my work.

The evening prayers were performed well. Mom was gushing about how great all the food was. I went up to find Jasmine to give her evening meal of puffed rice. She was missing. I called mom and got the helpers to search for her, they could not find her. I was terribly upset that something might have happened to her. I started crying when there was no evidence of the bird. Mom admonished me for crying over a pigeon, I felt like the bird flying away was an inauspicious sign of things to come.

Chapter 25 – Basil Leaf

Jasmine, the pigeon never did come back. She had probably gone to the retreat. I mailed Rupa about the disappearance of the bird. She responded quickly that even the '*Bird*' leaving was a clear sign that I was getting too attached to it. I had no time to spend mourning because the day after the bird disappeared, I had a call from a Wedding Planner. They were eager to hire me to do '*Menus*' for their weddings and called me in for an interview with an in house cookery demonstration to be done. It was ironic, that I had no man but a job prospective with a Wedding Planner.

My parents were becoming more modern by the day. They were happy that I had got the call and encouraged me to go for the interview.

Papa's words were "Maybe you were supposed to take a different course in your life and marriage will fall into place at that time."

Grandma blessed me and wished me luck. Mom, well I had to stop her calling up relatives to tell them about the job offer. I had to try to make it first. Anish was happy that if I did get the job, I would move to Chennai with him. Nandini, well she had been missing in action for some time after her brother-in-law's wedding. My parents and grandma went for it. I politely declined and no one forced me to attend it.

I was packing my bag for two-night trip to Chennai, when someone barged into my room. It was Nandini.

"So you want to go and play cook for some outsider? My in-laws are terribly upset about you going for the interview," Nandini spat out.

146 *Spices Are Sweet*

"Your in- laws, what do they have to do with my interview? I told mom not to tell anyone," I said.

"How can you offend me? My in- laws are upset that they have married into a family, which has a public cook. Now, no one will marry you. Papa just says yes to your ideas."

"What is your problem Nandini? I never did understand what the problem was. Your in- laws have no right if I even decide to take up pole dancing," I screamed.

Nandini slapped me hard on my cheek. I held my cheek in horror and burst out crying.

"You are too rebellious, how dare you talk to me like that," she shouted.

Mom and grandma came rushing into the room. They had obviously heard the war cry. I was crying.

"Why did you hit her?" glared grandma taking my hand from my cheek. "It's so red."

"Oh no , why did you hit her Nandini? Even I don't hit her," said mom sobbing.

"I really wished that we could be sisters Nandini, but you are too vicious." I said slowly rubbing my cheek.

"I hate you; I hated you the day you were born. You always had what you wanted. You studied well; you went to college. You are getting a job for what I do every day, cooking. I hate you," she spat out.

"Leave the room; I don't want you to interfere with Santhoshi except apologize. Go," said grandma firmly.

I was scared hearing grandma's steely voice; Nandini looked a bit scared. She walked off with my mother following her sobbing.

"She is jealous. Stay away from her," said grandma patting my head.

I lay down on her lap and cried for the relationship that had never been and would never be with the only sister I had.

Late that night, Papa was updated about the slapping incident. Nandini, who had come over to spend the night at our house, had returned to her place.

"I am very upset about what happened. Your mother should not have told her. When I was young I had to deal with many hateful people like this," papa said.

"She is our daughter," mom whispered, obviously not meaning me.

"She is a monster," corrected grandma.

Next morning, I was ready to head to the station. Nandini was back with a sorry face. She had been called by Papa.

"I am sorry," she said looking down at the floor.

I did not answer, I bid bye to the others and left. Anish picked me up from the station. He had an update about his college life. I was quiet, I remembered my last trip to the city and how things had changed since that time. I did not know whether I would get married soon, but I did know that I wanted my interview to work out.

The interview was brilliant. It was a young crowd. They loved the little variety I had prepared. I made a sweet *laddu* and *rasam*. Just that bit had impressed them. I was offered a decent salary and only had to make different menus for them. I did not even have to do the cooking; they had cooks who would do everything. I had to do recipes, just taste them; they would help launch my recipes into a book.

It was a dream job. At home, all were thrilled that it had been easy. Anish was out that night with his friends. He was making skilful use of his newfound freedom.

I had not spoken to Maya or Priya in a long time. Everyone was busy with their own lives. So much had changed, that I was dealing with things better. I was surprised to see Karthik's number blink on my screen.

"Welcome to Chennai," he said.

"How did you know?" I replied.

"Vidya told me, your cousin mentioned that you were coming

148 *Spices Are Sweet*

into Chennai this weekend. We are here too, would love to meet you for dinner," he said.

"Oh," I said.

"Is that all you have to say? How are you? I hear that you are a very well known cook, and very popular. Who would have thought that you could cook?" he laughed.

"I am fine. How are you? How is your wife?" I said slowly. Really, this was unexpected for him to call and invite me for dinner.

"You can find out in half an hour, we will pick you from the apartment? Yes," he said.

"Yes fine," I said hanging up.

I had to get ready quickly. I was touching up my make up when I heard my mobile ring. I rushed down to find Karthik in the front seat. He got out and said hi. I was going to hug him and stopped myself short. He looked well; he had gained weight.

"You look great," he said looking a bit taken aback.

"Hi Vidya," I said getting into the back seat.

"Hi Santhoshi, the new super chef," Vidya said rolling her eyes and giving me the once over.

Karthik was in the front seat and giving direction to the driver to take us to a new Italian Restaurant, Basil Leaf.

"How are you Vidya?" I asked her.

"I am happy, with good news," she patted her stomach.

"Congratulations. That was quick."

"Well you know Santhoshi; we should have kids in our twenties. Your fertility drops as you grow older," she said with a smug smile.

I just sat there dumbly. If Karthik heard this comment, he did not acknowledge it. Vidya was carrying her dress style with ease, *shalwar* with polka dots.

"So when are you getting married? Any proposals," she asked with her eyes doing the jig.

"Nothing," I said slowly, looking out of the window.

I had not even found a man yet to be hitched, and my fertility rate was the least of my concerns. I had not thought that far. Vidya pregnant? I hope the poor baby does not get blessed with her ogle eyes or her mean ways and definitely with her dress sense.

"I talk to Maya often," interrupted Karthik. "She is doing well, and she has met her guy."

"Mmhem," I replied.

I was hiding my shock exceptionally well. I had no clue that Karthik was in touch with Maya and she had met a guy. Our brief conversations were anything but warm.

"You have become so quiet," said Karthik.

"Santhoshi was a chatterbox in childhood, so she has settled at least in that," said Vidya.

Thankfully, we were at the Restaurant without further ado. I was wishing I were somewhere else. I got off the car and Vidya was still inside waiting for the driver to open her door. Then she proceeded to walk, ever so slowly, and painfully. Karthik was fussing over her and holding her hand.

"You ok, do you want to sit?" he asked her.

We had got off the car just now; I wanted to scream. She is pregnant and not had a brain surgery. After her slow, tortoise style walking into the lift, after everyone had made room for her. She was making such a show of getting into it. I wanted to go and push her in. We were seated in the restaurant.

I get a text message on my mobile. I was startled to see Karthik's message blinking "Don't order any wine. She does not approve alcohol. Please."

I deleted the text and looked up to see Vidya's protruding her eyes some more, and staring at my earrings.

"Let me order for all. I usually order for Karthik," jumped in Vidya.

150 *Spices Are Sweet*

Insulting, that she did not even ask me if I had any preferences. Well, I just wanted the night to end.

"How are your parents?" asked Karthik.

Vidya snapped her fingers at the waiter. I was shocked and turned to look at Karthik who was expectantly waiting for my reply. He was not even going to tell her off.

"Why did you snap your fingers at the waiter Vidya? It's offensive," I said.

The waiter appeared by our table and Vidya stared at me, ignored the question and started ordering. I turned to look at Karthik and he was fascinated with the floor. So, he was not going to stop her behaving like an idiot.

"So how are your parents?" asked Vidya patronizingly.

"How is your job Karthik," I asked ignoring her completely.

Vidya was annoyed and started moving the cutlery loudly and sulking.

"It's good," he stuttered. "Are you ok Vidya? Can I get you some juice?"

She did not answer, but just grunted and sulked. The dinner did not get any better. We did not have any conversation; we just sat there like a sore bunch of losers. The food came quickly; it was a pizza and pasta. The waiter served me first, plunked it on Vidya's plate like how they do in a prison and did not bother serving Karthik.

"What is this Karthik? The service is so bad," complained Vidya.

I took a few bites of pizza and played around with the pasta.

"Karthik, just one piece, is enough for you," Vidya said and took a pizza from his hand and gulped it.

Karthik looked like a kid, whose lollipop, had been taken away by a mean kid. She took everything from his plate and ate it. He looked hungry. No wonder he was putting on weight. He must be eating on the sly.

"Karthik, I am not feeling well. So let's skip dessert and I want to go home," I said.

"I want to eat dessert," said Vidya.

"You eat, I will catch a cab. Thanks for dinner," I said taking my purse out.

"Wait, the driver can drop you. No, don't take out money. This is our treat," he said.

"Bye Karthik. Take care Vidya," I said waking out quickly.

"She is so rude, walking out like that. She has not changed. No wonder she is not married," Vidya said loudly for the diners to hear. I walked out to the main road, hailed a three-wheeler, and got home. I was upset at meeting them.

I got home to find another text from Karthik, "You shouldn't have left like that. Vidya did not eat dessert; she was upset. She has invited you for lunch tomorrow."

Vidya ate enough of the main meal to provide a portion for a starving nation. Her health would have done some good without dessert, I thought. I was becoming mean. I slept fitfully that night, considering the disastrous evening. The only piece of disturbance was Vidya polishing of some hundreds of pizzas and cookies, a nightmare. Oh and yes, I did not reply to Karthik or answer his seven missed calls.

152 *Spices Are Sweet*

Chapter 26 - Cardamoms

The next morning dawned bright and early. I had planned to meet a tailor, thanks to what I saw in a magazine, to get some new work wear stitched. My wardrobe was changing to more traditional office wear. The tailor was a lovely woman, who helped me pick up beautiful ethnic fabric, to stitch them into comfortable Indian Pants and Tunics.

I was starving after spending two hours with the tailor. It was time to stop by at the new restaurant I had seen in the same magazine and have something to eat. It was a Garden theme, which boasted a beautiful garden filled with tall coconut trees, shrubs, and rose plants. The heady aroma of rose was enticing. A beautiful patio was set with tables for dining.

Entering, I was distracted by a poster for an exhibition that was happening in the hall. I walked in looking at paintings, jewellery and clothes. I bought a dozen bangles and earrings. The rumble in my stomach gently made me stop purchases and try out the restaurant.

A waiter approached me, "Madam, there is a table reserved for you, please this way."

"No, I did not reserve, there must be a mistake" I said.

"Sir, over there asked me to direct you to that table. Anyway the restaurant is full, so if you could, please," the waiter said walking towards a table.

I saw the silhouette of a man seated, I had no idea who it could be. I hope it's not Karthik, I thought for a moment. I was taken aback, when I saw it was Santhosh, the guy who had come to see me briefly, two days before to fix his rotten luck.

"Hi! I saw you walk into the exhibition. I thought I was seeing things, but no, it was you. Hope you will join me for lunch?" Santhosh was seated looking flustered.

"Santhosh?" I stammered.

"The restaurant is full, you won't be able to get a table, you could sit here," he continued.

The waiter pulled out the chair and smiled at me. I realized I should have reserved a table; the place was packed. Tables of aunties were staring over at me quizzically.

"Ok. Listen you take this table. I will get lunch somewhere else. I live in Chennai and I can come anytime," said Santhosh getting up.

"No uhm don't do that," I said sitting.

The waiter sighed and left me with a menu. Santhosh looked decent without any mud on him.

"I am sorry; I told the waiter if you walked in to bring you here. The place is always full. I thought we could just have lunch. I owe you an apology for coming to your house that day. I had no idea. I should be smart about it, after all the lies my mom and aunt told me to take me. I didn't think…," he rambled.

I smiled, "I have been there, done that. Don't worry about it."

"I had a meeting close by with a client and decided to stop by here for a salad. When did you come to Chennai? I was shocked to see you so soon."

"Just two days ago, I came for a job interview. I read a review about this place and this being my last afternoon in Chennai, I thought I would use it to do something useful," I replied.

"Check the menu, let's order. They take ages to serve," Santhosh gestured.

I looked at the menu and wondered if it was ok having lunch with this guy, whom I had met briefly back home. Oh well, he could not pounce on me just now. I looked up to see him staring at his menu intently. He looked ready to pounce on the menu if anything. I giggled, and he looked up quizzically. I quickly

154 *Spices Are Sweet*

looked down. He must have thought I was mad. We ordered some food and sugarcane juice.

I told him about the interview and the job. He told me about his work and family.

"It's very strange that I saw you that day in your house and today here," he said.

"I know I have had such strange few months. Nothing fazes me out," I replied.

The conversation flowed easily, and the lunch was delicious. Santhosh was stubborn that I should not pay and suggested that I could take him out the next time I was in Chennai. I stopped short and looked at him. He blushed and stared back at me. I thanked him and decided it was time to leave. There was a pot of cardamoms and cloves to munch on, natures mouth fresheners', left with the bill. We both took a few and said goodbye. On my way back home, I realized I had not even taken his number or given my number to him. There was no way I was going to pay him back for the lunch. It was better in a way; I had met far too many people these days.

I absently pulled a strand of my hair; the smell of Jasmine was still there. The cup was overflowing with studies and the job. I had to concentrate on getting things right this time.

Chapter 27 - Five Spices

A year later

New York!

I felt scared waiting for the doctor to call me in. The only sound was the assistant tapping on the keyboard. I looked at the empty waiting room and was thankful that there was no one else here. Did this secretary with the beautiful, calm face wonder what I was doing here? Will she read my report or will she be the one typing it? She looked up and smiled at me. She must have felt my eyes on her. I smiled back and flicked the magazine in my hands.

When he made this appointment and insisted, I should go; I felt sick in my stomach. My parents they would be so upset. My friends they would not have allowed me to go for the appointment. My relatives, they would have a day of gossip, when they heard about this. That's why I had not told a soul. Here, I was sitting alone petrified of my future.

I shook my head straight, and thought why I always think of what others think. What do I feel about all this? I don't want to be here at this appointment, where I have come half-an- hour early. I have not been able to sleep, since the day he gave me the appointment and asked me to go for this. He thinks I need help, he has thought so for some time now. I know for a fact that I don't need help, that I am a fairly normal person.

I thought back about our fights in the past. My suggestion for counselling was quickly dismissed, but here I am sitting at a private clinic today because he feels so. I closed my eyes tight and opened it and stared at the dark end of the corner. The

156 *Spices Are Sweet*

serene Buddha statue was at one end. I felt the soft flutter of a breeze slowly encircle me. I felt the trepidation in my mind clear. I don't need to be here for this appointment. I don't have to care what other people think of me.

He is the one who needs help more than me. His mood swings and personality disorders were so obvious. I was tired of trying to please him. If anyone needs to see a psychologist, it would be him. I took my mobile out and called him.

"Are you nervous baby?" he asked.

"I am nervous for you Ajay. I am not meeting the psychologist, if anyone needs help around here that's you. So I suggest you get here and meet the doctor. I am leaving for India for my friends wedding," Priya slammed the phone. She had packing to do and a flight to catch, sooner the better.

Bangalore.

"We need to take a break, I feel like I am tied to you," he said taking in a long deep smoke.

Maya felt a heavy stone being lifted from her heart, a relief like never before. It was time to make amends; she had to go to the wedding.

"That's the best thing I have heard love, let's take a break!" Maya replied picking up her bag.

"That's it? I said a mini break!" he continued looking up in shock.

"It's over; I have a wedding to attend in a week. Good bye!" Maya hurried to leave.

The past year was wasted time with a man, who was obsessed with running her life. It felt great to break free and leave. She had amends to make to her friend.

A Village in South India!

It was one big Indian Wedding again. We were in the splendid wedding hall, next to our family temple in the village. The theme was close to my heart, my very favourite "Jasmine". The decoration in Round Jasmine flowers, which were strewn in long garlands on the wall, decked the street with sweet fragrance. The hall was decorated in silk material and flowers. The soft sound of the clarinet felt gentle to the ears. The food should be delicious; I had planned the menu. The wedding planner group was all over the place.

My family of close and extended relatives, friends, the village, the astrologer and a whole lot of people who we did not know had arrived for the big event. . .

The bride, well she is slightly crazy I guess. I checked my makeup, which had been, carefully done at the salon. My aunt did talk about her being good luck for weddings, and wanted to tamper with my face. I had to decline politely. I mean I did not want to look like JOJO the clown at my wedding, did I?

My red kanjeevaram sari was as bright as the mehendi in my palms. I held up my hands to look at the deep red colour.

"When the mehendi is that deep red colour, it means your husband will love you forever!" whispered grandma.

I turned around with a smile and her eyes glistened with tears of joy. We hugged each other.

I guess you are not shocked, are you? At last, I am hitched; yes, we cut off the long courtship with Santhosh. I know you guessed it was him. There was no courtship. It was an arranged marriage except for our lunch tryst that no one knows about yet. Santosh has great fun teasing my mom that she never offered a glass of water the first day he visited us. Papa, well he was proud. There was a tear in his eye, when he gave me away in marriage.

Nandini and her in- laws, they attended, and complained about everything. The food was not good. The jasmines were pompous.

Karthik and Vidya came with their baby who was as grumpy as she was. I had met many babies in my life, but this baby would not smile, just stared at my earrings. Karthik, well what I felt is that some men are destined to live an unhappy marriage in

158 *Spices Are Sweet*

slavery. Vidya, her eyes had somehow grown very wide and she scared Santhosh with her questions and her staring.

Santhosh, he is a normal sort of bloke, who even tolerates grandma singing. I like to think that we were linked with our names and in previous birth. Everyone loved the fact that we gave them five spices as a return gift.

The best part of the wedding was having my family and my two friends Maya and Priya, who seemed to have grown up so fast in the past year. I made a promise that I won't become a new wife, no communication person. You know the kind, who gets married and forgets theirs friends for the first year. Well, I wouldn't do that would I?

Epilogue

Garlands made of fresh flowers: The exchange of garlands by the bride and groom is performed three times. This is to symbolize the acceptance of the fragrance of the other as well as to depict it is two bodies, but one soul.

The bride's right hand is placed in the groom's right hand and then tied together with a red cloth. They would walk around the sacred fire homam three times.

"Sapthapadhi": The first seven steps taken by the groom and the bride are vows to respect their journey in marriage.

First step: To respect and honour each other and live a prosperous Life.

Second step: To share each other's joy and sorrow and develop their physical, mental and spiritual powers.

Third step: To trust and be loyal to each other and earn a righteous living to increase their wealth.

Fourth step: To cultivate appreciation for knowledge, values, sacrifice and service by mutual love, respect, understanding and faith.

Fifth step: Vow of purity, love, family duties by praying to be blessed with healthy, honest and brave children.

Sixth step: To follow principles of Dharma (righteousness). They pray for self-control of the mind, body and soul and a long marital relationship.

Seventh step: To nurture an eternal bond of friendship and love by being true and loyal for a lifetime.

160 *Spices Are Sweet*

Stepping on the stone: The bride places her right foot on a grinding stone to symbolize that she can stand strong at all times in life. Silver toe rings are placed, on the second toe of the feet of the bride, by the groom, to signify that their love will remain forever, and the groom would look after and protect her.

"Arundhathi Star": The groom would show the bride the star "Arundhathi" in the sky. This small star belongs to the constellation of *Saptha Rishi* and is a double star attached to the star Vasishta. Legend, says that "Arundhathi" the wife of Vasishta was an example of an ideal wife. The two stars are double stars that move together, and the couple looking at the star, should also live a life of togetherness.

Blessings: The priests, elders of the family, friends and guests would shower flower petals and bless them to live a happily married life

The first meal: The bride and groom would be served their first meal in a banana leaf. They would feed each other sweets to mark their first meal together. The meal would be only a complete vegetarian extravaganza.

Lunch Menu: Sweets: Payasam (Sweet Rice pudding)

Laddu, Sweet Boli

Mains: Plain Rice, Chapathi, Vegetable Rice

Accompaniments: *Papad, Curd Raitha, Bheans Dhal Usili, Poriyal, Sambar, Rasam, Kulambu, Avial, Pachadi, Dhall, ghee, Pickle and chips*

Nalungu: Simple games that were developed by ancestors to get the groom and bride to get a little closer to each other. In olden times, mostly the bride and groom would meet only on the wedding day, this is changing in modern times and they get to meet and talk to each other. The games are always a fun time, with the bride's family and groom's family supporting each.

The groom would apply sandalwood paste and vermillion on the bride's forehead. The bride would apply the same on groom's hands.

A coconut is held by closing the groom's fingers around it, and the bride would try to remove the coconut from his hand. It is repeated by the bride and almost always, the groom wins by taking the coconut away from her hand.

The bride circles papads around the grooms head and tries to crush the *papad* on his head, the groom would have to move away.

The newlyweds play catch with flower balls.

A ring is put into a pot of water and the bride and the groom are asked to put their right hands into the water and find the ring. The person who finds the ring is proclaimed a winner.

The games are also a symbolic to show that a marriage works as a team.

Arathi: A solution of vermillion with torn up betel leaves is prepared on a plate. The plate is circled around the couple and the liquid is thrown away outside the entrance, to ward off evil eyes on the couple.

www.leadstartcorp.com

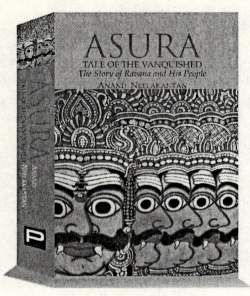

History is written by the Victors,
Ramayana belonged to Rama,
now Ravana is back to tell you his story –

ASURA
TALE OF THE VANQUISHED
The Story of Ravana and His People

Available at all Leading Bookstores and Book Selling websites
or by direct order from
LEADSTART PUBLISHING PVT LTD
Unit 122, Building B/2, Near Wadala RTO,
Wadala (E), Mumbai 400 037
T 91 22 2404 6887   W www.leadstartcorp.com

TITLES AVAILABLE

LEAP
Learning Empowerment & Achieving Potential

The LEAP series of books are tools of personal empowerment. They guide and assist individuals in the achievement of their full potential. While many goals are common to every human being, their achievement is an entirely individual journey...

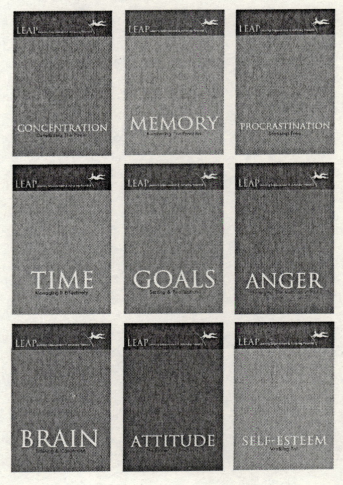